BATMAN BEYOND
RETURN OF THE JOKER ™

Novelization by MICHAEL TEITELBAUM

Based on the original story by PAUL DINI,
BRUCE TIMM, and GLEN MURAKAMI,
and the screenplay by PAUL DINI

Batman created by BOB KANE

SCHOLASTIC INC.

New York   Toronto   London   Auckland   Sydney
Mexico City   New Delhi   Hong Kong

*For Steven — a super hero fighting
the toughest battle of his life.*

*Thanks to Glen Murakami, Bruce Timm, and especially Paul Dini
for their marvelous story. To Charlie Kochman for his sharp eye
and generosity. May this be the first of many, Bud. To Beth
Dunfey for her input. And to Sheleigah, as always, for watching
the show with me. — M.T*

ISBN 0-439-20769-X

Designed by Peter Koblish

12 11 10 9 8 7 6 5 4 3 2 1   0 1 2 3 4 5 6/0
Printed in the U.S.A.
First Scholastic printing, November 2000

PROLOGUE

Terry McGinnis never had it easy.

When his parents split up he moved in with his father, Warren, but the two didn't get along very well. Terry was a free spirit who rejected his father's rules. Then Terry fell in with a tough crowd and ended up getting into trouble.

Meanwhile, Warren McGinnis was putting in long hours, working for Wayne-Powers Industries. The company had been built into a powerful international corporation by billionaire industrialist Bruce Wayne. But Wayne lost control of his company to Derek Powers, a greedy, corrupt businessman. When Warren uncovered a secret file showing that Powers was developing an illegal toxic nerve gas, Powers had him silenced by a criminal associate named Mr. Fixx.

On the night of Warren's death, Terry had argued with

his father and stormed out of their apartment. When he learned of his father's murder, Terry was wracked with guilt. He should have been there, he felt. He could have done something, maybe saved his father's life.

Terry had already stumbled upon Bruce Wayne's secret — the fact that he was the original Darknight Detective, the Batman. So Terry snuck into the Batcave and borrowed Wayne's superpowered Batsuit. Wayne hadn't used the suit since he stopped fighting crime as the Batman, over twenty years ago.

Using the Batsuit's incredible abilities, coupled with his own ingenuity, Terry McGinnis avenged his father's death and earned the respect of Bruce Wayne. Wayne then offered Terry a job — two jobs, really — one as his assistant, the other as the new Batman. Terry accepted both.

Young Terry McGinnis now fights crime in Gotham City. Through the Batsuit's built-in communications system, he is able to stay in contact with Bruce Wayne, so he can benefit from Bruce's knowledge, experience, and high-tech resources.

Terry McGinnis is the Batman of tomorrow — the Future Knight! He still doesn't have it easy, but he wouldn't want it any other way.

CHAPTER ONE

*R*OOOAAARRR!

The sleek black shape of the Batmobile sliced through the neon Gotham night. Unlike the earthbound Batmobile used by Bruce Wayne during *his* days as the Batman, this souped-up machine could fly. Dipping in and around the jagged electric skyline, the speeding craft made its way steadily toward the waterfront. Once a run-down, dangerous part of town frequented only by thieves and muggers, this section of the gleaming, high-tech city was now home to a series of huge industrial buildings.

Seventeen-year-old high school senior Terry McGinnis sat at the controls of the Batmobile. His thoughts turned, as they did each time he donned the enhanced Batsuit, to his father's murder. This was the key event in his life, and the turning point that brought him to his new role as Batman — the once and always protector of Gotham City.

Terry pushed these thoughts aside as a sprawling industrial building loomed before him. A neon sign atop it read GOTHAM SHIPPING. By day, this area was a bustling complex where technical equipment arrived in the city to be transported to its final destination. At night, it was a quiet, empty part of town, silently holding its breath until the first light of morning brought the chaos of commerce back once more.

Batman flipped a switch on the Batmobile's control console. The gleaming metal underbelly of the craft slid open, revealing the city below. Batman engaged the vehicle's autopilot, then leapt from his seat into the cool night air. His boot jets flared to life as he headed toward the imposing structure below.

In a small office just inside the main entrance of the Gotham Shipping building, a security guard leaned back on his dented metal folding chair. On most nights, the guard fought boredom rather than intruders. This night, however, would be different.

His feet resting on his tiny desk, the guard flipped through the day's *Gotham Globe* for the second time that evening. "Crime's up, the market's soaring, and the home team lost," he muttered to himself, tossing the newspaper aside. "So what else is new?"

A noise startled him. The guard leapt to his feet and pulled his laser weapon from its holster, then stepped out of the office. "Who's there?" he shouted, opening the building's main entrance. "This is private property. No trespassing allowed!"

Out of the darkness, a shaggy claw swiped at the guard, knocking the weapon from his hand and ripping several buttons off his uniform jacket in one swift motion. "Stay back!" the guard yelled, glancing down in horror at his torn clothing and empty hand.

The attacker came closer, stepping into a small pool of light shining from the office.

"W-What *are* you?" the guard stammered, getting his first look at the intruder.

The half-human, half-hyena creature that stood before him let out a shrill cackle that echoed eerily through the cavernous building.

The guard turned to run, but the creature was too fast. It bared its needle-sharp teeth and flashed its razorlike claws, then sprang forward, knocking the guard to the ground.

The fur-covered beast sniffed the unconscious guard like a dog surveying a potential meal, then turned around to face its companion.

A tall, gangly figure wearing clown makeup and a pointed witch's hat looked down at the motionless guard. "You should have told Woof here to 'heel'!" he joked.

"Hey, Ghoul," a gruff voice called out. "This thing is really hard to move!"

In the building's main warehouse, a thick-fingered brute operated a hover-lift. The flying forklift worked like a pair of floating mechanical hands, grabbing a huge control console. The brute, whose face was also covered in clown makeup, pulled a lever on the hover-lift. The massive mechanical hands ripped the giant console from its housing. But as the hover-lift tried to back away, the console got caught on two other delicate pieces of machinery.

"Slag it!" shouted the gruff-voiced brute as he struggled to remove the console without tipping the hover-lift.

"Stay cool, Bonk," Ghoul shouted to his teammate. "I'll send some help."

From the shadows, twin girls came bounding and tumbling like acrobats toward Bonk's hover-lift. They were both dressed in identical clown makeup, halter tops, and floppy hats. Executing perfect handstands, then cartwheels, the twins leapt high into the air, landing on either side of Bonk.

"Bonk's really got a delicate touch with this hover-lift, don't you think, Dee-Dee?" asked one of the girls sarcastically.

"Yeah, Dee-Dee," replied the other girl. "Delicate like a moose!"

The two Dee-Dees grabbed the hover-lift's controls and gently moved its metal claw. Within seconds, the control console cleared the machinery that had blocked it, and the lift backed away smoothly.

Bonk scowled first at one Dee-Dee, then the other. "I hate ripping off this big, heavy stuff," he snarled. "Give me cash cards to steal any day."

A second hover-lift pulled up alongside Bonk's. At its controls sat a heavyset man, also wearing clown makeup. "Zip it, Bonk!" he ordered. "The plan is to get in, grab the console, and get out fast."

"Okay, Chucko," Bonk replied. "You're the leader of this little mission."

Woof, Ghoul, Bonk, the Dee-Dees, and Chucko were all members of the criminal gang known as the Jokerz. They were fashioned after the original Joker — longtime enemy of the first Batman and the scourge of Gotham City thirty years before. These modern-day descendants dressed like demented clowns, following in the footsteps of the criminal madman from whom they took their name.

Chucko maneuvered his hover-lift around to the front of Bonk's, then used the mechanical arms on his vehicle to grab one end of the console. As he was doing so, Chucko caught a flash of movement out of the corner of his eye, more shadow than substance. Before he could react, a tall black figure smashed through a window behind him, slamming him from his hover-lift and sending him crashing to the floor below.

Batman landed on top of the control console. He brushed shards of window glass from his shoulders, then turned to Bonk and the Dee-Dees.

"It's a school night, boys and girls," Batman said. "I'm going to have to call your folks."

Bonk grabbed the controls of the hover-lift and yanked them violently.

"Bonk, don't!" the Dee-Dees shouted together, but the hover-lift lurched to one side. Both girls lost their footing and had to struggle to keep from falling.

Batman locked his magnetic boots into place and stood firmly as Bonk shook the console back and forth. "Yeah, Bonk. Don't!" he mimicked the Dee-Dees, smiling.

This enraged Bonk even further. He growled like a cornered animal.

Batman activated a mechanism hidden in the wrist of his Batsuit. Silently, as if the thought alone had triggered it, a Batarang appeared in his right hand. Terry McGinnis had gotten completely comfortable wearing the Batsuit. It now reacted to his thoughts and movements like a second skin. He tossed the flat, bat-shaped disk at Bonk, but it only glanced off the brute's heavily muscled body.

GRRR!

That's when Woof struck. The half-animal, half-human leapt at Batman from below, knocking him from the console.

OOMPFF!

Batman hit the floor hard, with Woof right on top of him.

"Yiiiiiiiiiiii! Hee-hee-hee-hee!" Woof shrieked, giggling maniacally.

Ghoul joined the fight next, grabbing Woof's leash and wrapping it around Batman's neck. Batman grabbed the leash with both hands, struggling to loosen the choke hold as Ghoul pulled the leather strap tighter.

Chucko scrambled back onto his hover-lift and started barking orders. "Let's go!" he shouted at Bonk. "Dee-Dee, open the door!"

Both Dee-Dees jumped from the hover-lift, executing perfect midair somersaults. They landed next to the control panel that operated the building's doors. One Dee-Dee used a handheld electric stun device to short out the building's security system. The other pulled a lever on the panel.

A large round door in the floor slid open. On the level below, a flatbed transport vehicle hovered a few feet off the ground.

The Dee-Dees bounded back up to the hover-lifts. The stolen control console floated slowly down through the circular opening in the floor.

Giving up hope of loosening the leash that cut into his neck, Batman reached over his head and grabbed Ghoul by the shirt. Lunging forward, he flipped Ghoul over his back, tossing him right into Woof. The two Jokerz tumbled over each other as Batman tore the leash from his throat and filled his lungs with air.

Woof and Ghoul ignored the Future Knight, jumped out through the window, and headed down a flight of stairs. Batman let them go. He dashed to the opening in the floor and dove through.

Dee-Dee spotted Batman coming right at her. "Incoming!" she shouted.

Batman landed behind Bonk, who turned and glared at the hero. "You got a death wish, Bats?" he shouted.

"Just being a good citizen," Batman replied.

Bonk flipped a switch on his hover-lift, opening its mechanical hands and releasing his end of the control console. He powered up the lift's rockets and veered away, carrying Batman with him.

Chucko's lift now supported the full weight of the enormous control console. "Bonk, you moron!" he screamed, struggling to keep his hover-lift airborne. "Get back here! I can't hold this thing by myself!"

Bonk left the pilot's seat and tackled Batman. As his hover-lift soared wildly out of control, the surprisingly agile Bonk was on top of the Future Knight in an instant. The two combatants crashed to the hover-lift's floor, Batman struggling in vain to gain the upper hand. Suddenly, the careening vehicle slammed into the warehouse wall. It swerved across the cavernous building, smashing into a set of windows and sending shards of shattered glass to the floor below.

Bonk forced Batman to the edge of the hover-lift. The hero's head hung upside down as the lift approached the side of the building. But through a garbled haze of pain, Batman spied something that made him smile.

"Flagpole," he mumbled, struggling to keep Bonk's fist from pounding him again.

"What's that you say, Bats?" Bonk shouted, moving his face close to Batman's. "You'll have to speak up!"

Batman nodded and raised his voice. "I said 'flagpole'!"

WHUMP!

A long flagpole jutting out from the side of the warehouse caught Bonk in the midsection, wrenching him from the hover-lift. Winded, Bonk dangled helplessly, hundreds of feet above the ground.

Instantly Batman sprang to his feet and grabbed the lift's controls, steadying the plunging vehicle. Then he shook his head quickly, trying to forget the physical pain he was experiencing and focus on the task at hand. Gunning the lift's accelerator lever, he shot toward Chucko's hover-lift.

Chucko, meanwhile, had just managed to gain control of his wobbly craft. But the vehicle strained under the weight of the control console it still grasped in its mechanical hands. Chucko glanced to his right and saw Batman streaking directly at him.

"He's coming this way!" Chucko shouted.

"Well, move then!" Dee-Dee screamed back.

"I can't!" Chucko barked angrily as Batman zoomed closer. "This machine is too heavy. I can barely hold on to it."

"Then drop it!" shrieked the other Dee-Dee.

Chucko glared at the Dee-Dees. He didn't like being told what to do. But it didn't take him long to figure out that Dee-Dee was right. He released the control console and veered his hover-lift away, narrowly missing the speeding Batman.

At the flatbed, Ghoul and Woof looked up, expecting to see the console floating gently toward the transport vehicle. Instead, the heavy machine was plunging right at them.

Ghoul and Woof screeched as they dove out of the way. The massive machine slammed into the transport, smashing both itself and the flatbed to bits. Ghoul immediately leapt onto the smoldering wreckage, rummaging through the smoking, sparking mess. Finally, he managed to pull a computer memory board from the console. *At least we'll have something to bring to the boss*, he thought.

Suddenly, a shadow from above crossed Ghoul's face. He looked up to see Batman gliding through the air on the Batsuit's retractable wings, his arms spread open wide. Ghoul tossed a smiley-face grenade at Batman, who shifted the course of his descent and dove out of the way.

THOOOM!

The grenade exploded in midair, its impact slamming Batman into the wall. Dazed but still conscious, he tumbled to the floor.

13

Chucko piloted his hover-lift over to Ghoul and Woof. "Let's go!" he shouted to his two shaken teammates. "Move it!"

Ghoul climbed onto the hover-lift, followed closely by Woof. They swooped past the flagpole where Bonk dangled, hanging on for all he was worth. As it passed beneath him, Bonk let go and dropped down. The tiny craft, wobbling from the weight of too many passengers, accelerated out of the building.

Batman pulled himself off the floor and looked around. The Jokerz were gone, but without what they had come for. Behind him the twisted hunk of wrecked console sparked brightly, then exploded into flames.

"This is definitely not coming out of *my* allowance!" he muttered to himself. Then he plunged back outside into the cool Gotham night, heading for the Batmobile.

CHAPTER TWO

Entering the Batcave still sent chills down Terry's spine. He had thought that by now he'd have grown used to the place. Maybe after many all-night research sessions at the Batcomputer with his teacher, boss, and mentor, Bruce Wayne, he would come to think of it as ordinary.

But he was wrong.

Like all kids his age in Gotham City, Terry grew up hearing stories about the legendary hero called the Batman, who fought crime not just on the rooftops and streets, but also from within the hidden secrecy of the mysterious Batcave. Terry still could not believe that he was actually the new Batman — that he was privy to the secrets, technology, and knowledge that resided deep inside the private lair. "Unbearably cool" is how Terry described the experi-

15

ence to Bruce Wayne. Not quite the words that the former Batman would have chosen.

Terry eased the Batmobile through the night sky, to the outskirts of town. Gleaming electric skyscrapers gave way to tree-covered mountains. Rising like a medieval castle from one such wooded expanse was Wayne Manor, home to the billionaire industrialist whose name it bore.

Terry guided the Batmobile toward the house, brushing the tops of a thick stand of pines as he began his descent. When the glossy ebony craft was only a few feet away, two huge pines swiveled in opposite directions, like the doors of a cabinet opening, revealing a sheer rock wall. A hidden stone door rose up into the rock wall, opening the secret entrance to the Batcave. Once the Batmobile had cleared the door, it quickly slid closed. Then the pine trees swiveled back into their proper position.

The Batmobile flew through a maze of dark tunnels. It had taken Terry several weeks to learn the one and only correct route. Bruce Wayne was a man who liked his privacy.

The sleek craft finally emerged from the maze and entered the Batcave's main chamber. Rough rock walls arched up to a tall, craggy ceiling high above. Terry gently brought the Batmobile to rest on its landing pad under the stalactites. Then he glanced around at the treasures, trophies, and souvenirs of triumphs and failures past that decorated the vast cave. In addition to the Batcomputer, there was a giant penny standing on its edge, a huge statue of a T-Rex, and several glass museum cases filled with weapons and costumes, each holding a story from the days when Bruce Wayne patrolled the Gotham City night.

One long case in particular caught Terry's attention, as it always did. The glass cabinet contained several compartments, each one holding a costume. Previous versions of the Batman costume — as well as the one worn by Robin, the Boy Wonder who had joined the original Batman on so many of his adventures — hung in the case, carefully displayed.

The final case stood empty, no longer holding the Batman costume Terry now wore. More than two decades ago Bruce Wayne had created the Batsuit to increase his own strength and athletic ability. It connected to the wearer's nervous system and worked like another layer of muscle. It also acted as a bulletproof shield against small-caliber ammunition.

Bruce had hoped the suit would prolong his years as Batman, and it did for a while. But eventually his aging heart couldn't take the strain of battling Gotham's worst criminals anymore, even with a souped-up Batsuit. And so he had retired, hanging up the costume next to the others in the display case, where it stayed until Terry entered his life.

Wrinkled, a bit hunched over, and easily winded, Bruce Wayne, now in his seventies, may have looked the part of a feeble old man. But his piercing eyes still burned with fire, and the cane he used to help him walk could be wielded, when necessary, as a most effective weapon.

As Terry climbed out of the Batmobile, he heard the unmistakable sound of a Batarang whizzing through the air. He followed the spinning blur, watching as it sliced the head off a dummy of Two-Face — one of the original Batman's most dangerous foes. Next to Two-Face stood dummies of several of Gotham's other legendary super-villains: the Riddler, Killer Croc, and Mr. Freeze. The Batarang circled the Batcave, then was crisply snatched out of the air by the wrinkled but steady hand of the man who had thrown it — Bruce Wayne.

Bruce nodded at his dog, Ace, a powerful Doberman, who sat nearby wagging his tail, enjoying the sight of his master in action. "I've still got it," Bruce said to Ace.

"You'll get no argument from me," Terry replied as he pulled off his mask, revealing a handsome, finely chiseled face and soft brown hair.

Bruce and Ace joined him near the Batmobile. "How did it go with the Jokerz?" Bruce asked in a flat, even tone.

"I broke up the robbery," Terry reported. "But something puzzles me. This is the third time this month that gang was trying to steal high-tech machinery like control consoles and guidance systems. It doesn't make any sense — the Jokerz don't use that stuff."

"They're probably fencing it," Bruce explained as the trio walked toward the center of the Batcave. "Corporate espionage is big business. There's a lot of demand for communications and guidance systems. The Jokerz stand to make a handsome profit if they can get their hands on the right equipment to sell."

"I'll sit tight until I can get another shot at them," Terry offered. "Maybe next time I can collar a few of them for Commissioner Gordon's collection."

Out of the corner of his eye, Terry caught a picture of Bruce on one section of the Batcomputer's main screen. It was part of a news broadcast, and Bruce Wayne was the top story.

"Today, Gotham billionaire Bruce Wayne stunned the financial world by announcing that he would resume active leadership of Wayne Enterprises," the computer-generated newscaster reported. "For the past several years Wayne has stayed out of the corporate spotlight, letting others run his company. But now he's back in charge. While most shareholders and employees welcomed this news, not everyone seems completely pleased about this turn of events. Here's company Operations Manager Jordan Pryce."

The image on the screen switched to that of a tall, thin man in his early fifties. Jordan Pryce sat comfortably, almost arrogantly, in his large, beautifully decorated office at Wayne Enterprises. "I, of course, join the rest of our Wayne Enterprises family in welcoming back Bruce Wayne," Pryce stated, trying hard, but failing, to sound happy about this development. "We can all profit from Mr. Wayne's years of experience. Still, the day-to-day pressures of running a huge corporation would be stressful even for a young man. I hope Mr. Wayne is up to the challenge."

"He's not *too* bitter, is he?" Terry asked.

"Pryce was planning on taking over the top spot at Wayne Enterprises," Bruce explained. "My return torpedoed any dreams he had of being the boss."

"Are you going to keep him around, knowing how he feels?" Terry asked, turning away from the screen.

"I will if he'll stay on my terms," Bruce replied. "He's sharp, a valuable employee. But I've fought hard to regain control of my family's company, and I won't hand it over again. Pryce does it my way or he can start e-mailing his resume."

Terry stroked his chin thoughtfully and looked around the Batcave. "So, with all the long hours you'll be putting in at the office," Terry began, "will you have less time for" — Terry held up the Batman mask — "you know."

Bruce smiled. Not something Terry had seen him do often. "Who sleeps anymore?" Bruce asked, shrugging.

The newscaster returned to the screen. "Wayne will officially take over the reins of the company later this week in a special ceremony at the recently completed Wayne Enterprises complex, a state-of-the-art office and science center." The image of an ultramodern glass tower flashed on the screen.

"Nice," Terry said, nodding at the picture.

"Even though I don't get around as much as I like, I can still help the city in some small ways," Bruce replied modestly.

"Small?" Terry asked, laughing. "There's nothing small about that building. It must have cost a billion bucks."

"Three billion, actually," Bruce corrected. "But who's counting?"

"I sure hope I'm in your will," Terry said half seriously, flashing Bruce his biggest smile.

Bruce patted Terry affectionately on the back. "I'm taking it all with me, kid," he replied flatly.

"Figures," Terry said, shaking his head. He yawned, then stretched. A sharp pain shot through his shoulder. "Oww!" he yelped, suddenly remembering how Woof had landed hard on top of him earlier that evening.

"You okay?" Bruce asked, concern showing in his voice.

"Yeah," Terry answered, heading to the changing room to switch into his street clothes. "It looks like the Jokerz are doing some genetic splicing these days. A crazed hyena-boy they created caught me off guard. Almost took a bite out of me. No way I could have explained *that* to Dana!"

Bruce glanced at his watch. He frowned, noting the late hour. "You're not going out *now*, are you?"

Terry stepped from the changing room wearing his jeans, T-shirt, and brown jacket. "The night is young," he announced, grinning, "and so am I."

"I think a good night's rest might be more beneficial," Bruce lectured in a fatherly tone.

Terry slipped the Batsuit into his backpack, which he then slung over his shoulder. Heading out of the Batcave, he turned back to Bruce. "Hey, like you said, who needs sleep?"

CHAPTER THREE

As Bruce Wayne had discovered many years earlier, leading a double life was not easy. Terry raced through downtown Gotham to meet his date at their favorite dance club. Rushing inside, he was immediately overwhelmed by the loud, throbbing music and bright flashing lights that crisscrossed the dance floor.

Terry slipped into a booth and scanned the floor for the girl he had been seeing for some months now, sure that she had arrived before him. She always did.

But as soon as he was seated, exhaustion from his recent battle flooded over him. His eyes closed, and before long he was snoring, head back, mouth open.

Terry's date — a pretty, dark-haired girl, dressed in a shimmering, sequined miniskirt and matching jacket — spotted him and rolled her eyes. Without missing a beat she danced over to the booth and pulled Terry to his feet. "Up and at 'em, Tiger," she said as Terry tried to shake the cobwebs from his head. "You can doze on Bruce Wayne's time, not mine!"

"Sorry, Dana," Terry muttered, forcing a smile and trying to move with the beat as best he could.

Dana Tan was one of the smartest and prettiest girls in Terry's high school. He loved her free spirit and sharp mind. Dana had little use for most of the boys in her class, but she was attracted to the simmering danger that seemed to lurk just beneath Terry's handsome exterior.

Dana was glad to see her boyfriend. She burst onto the dance floor, shaking her hips and swinging her arms. Terry tried to keep up, but he could barely manage to stay on his feet.

Dana had no idea that Terry was the new Batman. She *did* know that he worked as Bruce Wayne's assistant. She also knew that his work for the billionaire included lots of late nights and many unexplained cell-phone calls that pulled him away from their dates.

"Great song, huh?" Dana asked, trying to engage him in some kind of conversation.

"Huh?" Terry grunted. "Oh, yeah. Great."

Dana didn't want to tie Terry down. She respected his apparent need for freedom too much. She just wished he would open up more and share some of the mysterious parts of his life with her. But that was unlikely. Long ago, Bruce Wayne had learned the value of keeping that part of his life a secret. This was one of the first lessons he'd impressed upon his young apprentice.

Dana leaned close to Terry's ear and pointed to her friend Blade dancing nearby with a weird-looking guy.

"Check out the loser Blade's with," Dana whispered, pinching her nose with two fingers. "P.U.!"

"Uh-huh," Terry agreed, fighting to keep his eyes open.

Dana frowned, realizing that Terry really wasn't paying attention. "Ter, my head is on fire," she said, testing him. "See the big flames shooting out?"

"You look good," he replied, clearly not registering what Dana had just told him. In a daze, he accidentally started dancing with another girl.

"McGinnis!" Dana shouted over the blaring music.

Terry's head straightened up, and he moved back over to Dana. "Uh, sorry, babe," he apologized, trying to get back into the dance rhythm. "Guess the day was longer than I thought."

Dana took Terry's hand and led him back to the booth. "Let's sit this one out," she told him, sighing. She flagged down a waitress. "Coffee, please. And leave the pot."

Not all of Gotham had been rebuilt into a shining, ultra-modern city of tomorrow. A few neighborhoods had been left to deteriorate. A crumbling factory in one such run-down section was the former home of the Jolly Jack Candy Company. The faded JOLLY JACK sign painted on the front of the building could still be seen, but the candy company had gone out of business long ago.

However, this did not mean that the factory was empty. Far from it.

The inside of the building had been converted into the Jokerz headquarters. The main floor looked like a bizarre cross between a Gothic castle and an expensive toy store. The gang had recently returned from their failed attempt to steal the control console from the Gotham Shipping building. They now stood before their leader, who sat at one end of a long table, hidden in shadows.

Chucko stared down the length of the table toward the leader's eyes, which gleamed through the darkness. "Batman showed up so we had to ditch the console," Chucko explained. "We *were* able to save this." He pulled out the computer memory board he had taken from the wrecked console and slid it down the length of the table. "I know it's not much, but —"

"It's not much?" interrupted the shadowy figure. His purple-gloved fist smashed the memory board to bits. On the table next to the leader sat a jar of Jolly Jack jelly beans. The jar skidded a few inches with the impact of the blow. "It's nothing! And you are all a bunch of sad losers! A disgrace to the name 'Joker'!"

The leader glared at the group before him. "You're nothing but a gang of rank amateurs. Kids. Why in *my* day —"

Bonk stepped forward, interrupting. "In *your* day!" Bonk snarled. "Ever since you conned your way into this gang, all we've heard is 'your day *this*' and 'your day *that*.'"

"Bonk," Chucko said, raising his hand, trying to warn his teammate that this confrontation could not possibly have a happy ending.

Bonk shoved Chucko's hand away. He was on a roll, and not about to stop. "Your day is over, old man," Bonk continued, leaning in close to the leader. "Even if you *are* who you say you are. Although, personally, I think you're a fake!"

The shadowed figure took a jelly bean from the jar and leaned back in his seat. The faint hint of a smile was just visible. "Ah," the leader sighed. "It's a brave new world that has such amateurs in it." He tossed the candy into his mouth.

Bonk turned to the rest of the Jokerz, looking for support. "He's got us running around ripping off a lot of geek-junk, but no cash. He won't tell us what his plan is, *if* he even has one. Well, I for one want out!"

The leader lifted a strange-looking weapon and pointed it at Bonk. "If you insist," the dark figure said, taking aim.

Bonk's expression changed instantly. He began to sweat. "Hey man, t-take it easy," he stammered. "I was just kidding."

The leader fired the weapon. A flag that said *BANG!* popped out. "I was kidding, too," he said.

The Jokerz let out a collective sigh of relief.

Their leader smiled a cold, thin grin. Then a slender dart flew from the flag and struck Bonk, slamming him onto the long table.

The shadowy figure stood up, then stepped into the light. A broad grin filled his chalk-white face, and his oily green hair shone in the light. The original Joker, Batman's all-time greatest enemy, stared in mock sympathy at Bonk. "Oops, my mistake. I *wasn't* kidding."

Bonk gasped in shock as his pained faced twisted into a hideous version of the Joker's trademark grin. As the toxic venom spread, he grabbed his jaw in agony. Then his head dropped back, lifeless.

"That's also how we did it in my day!" the Joker cackled. He strode toward the remaining Jokerz, hands clasped behind his back. The gang members backed away, terrified.

"Y'know, kids, a lot has changed while your old uncle Joker was away," he began, looking right at the frightened group. "New Gotham, new rules — even a new Batman." The Joker spread his arms wide and smiled enthusiastically. "But now I'm rested and ready to give this old town a wedgie again — Joker style!"

The Jokerz looked at one another hopefully. Perhaps they were not all about to suffer Bonk's fate.

"But I have to know you're with me," the Joker implored. "Will you say it for me one time?"

"We're with you!" the five remaining gang members all shouted quickly.

"A little louder," the Joker requested.

"WE'RE WITH YOU!" the Jokerz screamed at the top of their lungs.

The Joker stepped between the Dee-Dees, putting an arm around each one. "Dee-Dee?" he asked.

"WE'RE WITH YOU!" both girls shouted.

The Joker cornered Chucko and Ghoul. He was clearly enjoying this show of power. "How about you boys?"

"WE'RE WITH YOU!" the two Jokerz yelled in strained voices.

"Woofie-baby?" the Joker asked, leaning down close to Woof.

The half-man, half-hyena just licked the boss's face.

"Aww!" the Joker cooed. "I'll take that as a yes." Then he stood up and surveyed his troops. "Well, your renewed faith puts a smile in my heart. Let's forget tonight's mishap and start over."

"Great idea, boss!" Chucko agreed instantly.

The Joker grinned, then turned to Ghoul. "Now, down to business. Ghoul, my boy, we're going to need another tracking control console like the one you all bungled tonight. Find out who's got one they'd be willing to donate to our little organization."

Ghoul nodded, then typed away on a computer keyboard. A list of names popped up on the monitor. "What we're after is a cutting-edge tracking device," Ghoul explained, pointing to the on-screen list. "These are the only other places we'd find one."

The Joker leaned in toward the screen and read down the list. "No, nope, uh-uh, no, not them. Ah, wait a minute." The Joker smiled wickedly and pointed to a name on the list. "That's it!"

Ghoul looked up at the Joker. The shock registered on his face. "There?" he exclaimed. "The Wayne Enterprises complex? Security there is going to be really tight!"

"Yes," the Joker snickered, his evil smile growing even broader. "But think of the fun we'll have!"

CHAPTER FOUR

The Wayne Enterprises complex towered above most of the other buildings in the luminous Gotham skyline. The enormous glass palace was the city's newest skyscraper. Bruce Wayne had spared no expense in the construction of the symbol of his international corporation.

A multilevel terrace, completely enclosed in glass, made up the top few floors of the building. During the day, visitors to the terrace walked among the clouds. At night, it seemed as if they could reach up and touch the stars.

Terry McGinnis stepped from the elevator and strolled into the crowd that had gathered on the terrace. The formal reception to celebrate Bruce Wayne's return to the top spot in his company was under way. Bruce was used to fancy, formal affairs like this one. He had been attending them for most of his adult life, either as a guest or as the host. For Terry, this was a whole new experience. Not used to wearing a tuxedo, he fiddled with his collar.

Two attractive young women pointed in Terry's direction. He flashed his biggest smile. *Maybe this won't be so bad after all*, he thought.

"He's adorable," the first woman said.

"So handsome," added the second.

That's when Terry saw Bruce enter the room behind him. *They're talking about Bruce!* he realized.

"Ladies," Bruce said softly, nodding at the two women. He then turned to Terry.

"Gotta be the money," Terry whispered to his boss.

"Right," Bruce admitted to Terry, smiling and nodding to several other party guests.

A woman in her mid-thirties wearing a business suit approached them. "Good evening, Mr. Wayne," she said. "So good to see you again."

Bruce nodded. "Ms. Carr. You remember my assistant, Terry McGinnis?"

"Of course," Ms. Carr replied, smiling. "I'm glad you could join us, Terry. This is a historic night. Everyone is here. Well, everyone except Mr. Pryce, unfortunately."

"That's no surprise," Bruce said to Terry with a wink.

Ms. Carr had made all the arrangements for the evening's affair. She now stepped up to a podium in the center of a long dais, where Bruce and the other dignitaries would be seated for the dinner. "May I have your attention, please," she said into the microphone. The crowd grew silent. "It is my pleasure to welcome back the guiding light of this company, Mister Bruce Wayne."

The terrace erupted into thunderous applause as Bruce moved to the podium. "Thank you, Ms. Carr," he began. "It's a pleasure to see you all again. In the future I hope to —"

CRAK-SCREEEE!

Static crackled, then a piercing whine interrupted Bruce, screeching through the public address system. Bruce waited for it to fade away, then continued. "Er, I was saying, I hope to spend time getting to know each member of our company, learning about you individually, and —"

SCREEEEEEEEE!!

The feedback came again, this time louder and lasting longer. The guests grabbed their ears. Bruce stepped back from the microphone as the screech changed into a sinister electronic laugh.

"HA-HA-HA-HA-HA!"

That's when the Jokerz struck. The Dee-Dees burst from their hiding places on either side of the room, tumbling toward the podium. Woof charged from the back of the terrace, growling savagely and rushing right for Bruce.

The crowd scattered in fear as Ms. Carr quickly called

security on her cell phone. "Security, emergency on the terrace level!"

In the building's nearby security station, a team of uniformed guards leapt to their feet and rushed to the door. "On our way," one of the guards shouted into his phone.

The security station's door slid open automatically. The guards skidded to a halt. "What the —" cried one of them.

Standing in the doorway were two clowns wearing gas masks. One was short and squat, the other tall and wearing a floppy hat. "Surprise!" the first one shouted as he tossed several gas grenades into the room. Within seconds, the security station was filled with thick, noxious smoke. The guards fell to the floor, unconscious.

Back on the terrace, Woof launched himself onto the dais, landing inches from Bruce Wayne's face. The beast snarled and growled, hoping to frighten the guest of honor. But Bruce held his ground. To him, this was just another punk. Hairy, with big teeth and sharp claws, but a punk nonetheless. With a quickness that startled the beast, Bruce slammed Woof with his cane, knocking the mutant to the floor.

Terry ran up to his mentor. "Are you going to be okay?" Bruce nodded. "Go to work," he said flatly.

Terry dashed away just as the Dee-Dees tumbled up to Bruce. Each girl grabbed one of his arms.

"Well, if it isn't old Mr. Wayne!" Dee-Dee cooed. "So debonair!"

"So dapper!" the other Dee-Dee added.

Bruce swung his cane in a wide arc, trying to reach both girls with one swift stroke. But they easily ducked out of the way. Then they struck as one, kicking Bruce in the midsection. He tumbled to the floor, gasping for breath.

The terrace began to shake. Water glasses on the dais tumbled over, mirrors on the wall cracked, and panic overtook the guests. A deep rumble filled the room, followed by thick smoke and flashing laser lights. Then a trapdoor in the dais silently slid open. A white-faced figure with green hair sprang into the room, laughing maniacally.

"Hello, Gotham!" he shouted. "The Joker's back in town! Ha-ha-ha-ha!"

Bruce caught his breath and scrambled to his feet, staring at the figure before him in disbelief. "It can't be," he muttered, the color draining from his face. His mind raced for a rational explanation, but found none. "It's impossible."

The Joker turned to face Bruce, his familiar grin spread wide across his face. "Oh, no, your old eyes do not deceive you, Brucie, old boy," the Joker cackled. He clearly was enjoying this. "After all, who'd know me better than *you*?"

As the Joker reached out a gloved hand to grab Bruce, Batman swooped down and tackled the crazed clown, slamming him to the floor.

"Back off, gruesome," Batman barked, rolling to his feet.

"Ah, the new boy in town," the Joker replied, looking Batman up and down. "The ears are too long and I miss the cape, but overall, not too shabby. Not bad at all." The Joker bounded to his feet and called out for Woof.

The fur-covered mutant vaulted to his boss's side.

"Sic 'im, doggie," the Joker ordered.

Woof launched himself onto Batman, teeth bared, claws slashing. As the Future Knight grabbed the freakish creature by the head, the two wrestled onto the floor.

The Joker turned away from the battle and spoke softly into a handheld communications device. "How's it coming down there, boys?"

In a research lab many stories below the elegant terrace, Chucko and Ghoul were hard at work. Operating a hover-lift, they grabbed a huge tracking control console, similar to the one they had tried to steal a few days earlier. "We're home free, boss," Chucko announced into his wrist communicator, at the same time swiftly maneuvering the console away from its housing.

"Then I'll see you there," the Joker's voice replied through the communicator's tiny speaker.

"Hang on!" Chucko shouted at Ghoul. "We're outta here!" Ghoul gripped the back of Chucko's seat as the hover-lift smashed through the door of the lab, the stolen console firmly in its powerful mechanical grasp.

Back on the terrace, Woof swiped at Batman with his front claws, pinning the Future Knight to the floor. The young hero flipped the snarling beast off with a powerful kick, then scrambled to his feet just as Woof leapt at him once more. With a crash, the two tumbled to the floor in front of the dais.

The Joker snapped his fingers. "Time to go, Dee-Dee," he announced, and the two sisters bounded to his side. Then the Joker pressed a button on a small remote. Within seconds, a purple hover-car with a giant clown face painted on the back floated up to the terrace. The Joker gave a short whistle and Woof instantly broke off his attack. The creature dashed for the car, followed by Dee-Dee and, finally, the Joker.

"You're not going to get away again!" Batman shouted. His boot jets flared on and he took to the air, closing in on the fleeing gang.

The Joker reached the hover-car first. As the others scrambled in, he pressed another button on his remote. A powerful explosion rocked the terrace, then another and another. Hidden explosive devices tore through the bar, the food table, and the podium as terrified guests raced for cover.

Batman glanced over his shoulder at the chaos and destruction behind him. Then he turned back to the Joker, who revved the engine on his hovering car.

"What's it going to be, Batfake?" the Joker called out. "Stop the bad guys or save the innocent victims?"

Batman knew he had no choice. Grimacing, he turned and fired his boot jets, streaking back to the screaming crowd. *THOOOM!*

Just then, a deafening blast tore a large section of railing off the edge of the terrace, pulling two horrified guests along with it. They plunged, screaming, down the outside of the immense glass tower.

Batman dove straight down after them, his boot jets lighting up the night sky. Before they had fallen ten stories, the Future Knight grabbed the petrified couple and flew them back up to the terrace.

The explosions had stopped. Bruce Wayne made it over to Batman, who scanned the night sky for a sign of the Jokerz. But the hover-car was gone, and only the thick smoke of the devastated terrace remained.

CHAPTER FIVE

The ride back to Wayne Manor was fraught with silent tension. To Terry, it felt as if it would last forever.

When he couldn't stand Bruce's stony silence any longer, Terry finally spoke up. "I know what you're thinking," the young man said uncomfortably. "You think I screwed up. I let the clown go in order to save those people."

"You did the right thing," Bruce replied firmly, his face a grim mask.

"So, the Joker, huh?" Terry asked, glancing at his mentor. Bruce remained silent.

"Looks pretty spry for a guy who's gotta be in his mid-eighties, right?" Terry continued. Bruce stared out the window. "Any theories on that? You know, clone? Robot? Suspended animation in a block of ice for all this time?"

"Shut up and drive," Bruce replied, his eyes firmly fixed on the road ahead.

Terry looked at his mentor in surprise, then shrugged and turned back to his driving. "Yes, sir," he said softly.

In a suburban neighborhood just outside Gotham City, a heavyset, middle-aged man sat on his couch. His feet rested on the coffee table as he watched the evening news. His house looked like many others on the street. Old but clean furniture decorated the den, family photos lined the walls, a few sports trophies collected dust on shelves.

The man stared intently at the TV, watching events that had taken place earlier that evening. A computer-generated newscaster on the screen spoke over footage of a gruesome scene. "This was the scene just three hours ago," the newscaster reported, "as a man claiming to be the legendary Joker disrupted a ceremony at the newly opened Wayne Enterprises building."

Sweat broke out on the man's forehead. Not revealing any emotion, he watched the Joker's dramatic entrance, Batman's struggle with Woof, and the explosions that had rocked the terrace.

A soft, sweet voice called to the man from another part of the house. "Tim? What are you watching?"

The man stared silently at the screen. He didn't reply as the images poured over him.

"Adding to the drama," the newscaster continued, "was the appearance of another Gotham icon, the Batman, who engaged his one-time foe in a stunning aerial battle."

"Tim?" the man's wife called again.

Tim shook his head, wiped the sweat with his sleeve, then hit the mute button on his TV remote. "It's nothing, sweetheart," he called back. "Just the news."

The Joker's face filled the screen. Sitting in silence, the man stared at the terrifying image, sweat reappearing on his brow.

Gotham City Police Commissioner Barbara Gordon stared at her computer monitor. The Joker's glaring face filled the screen. Commissioner Gordon thought of her younger days when, as Batgirl, she had fought crime in Gotham City side by side with Batman. She had shared Bruce Wayne's secret for all those years. Now, she knew of Terry McGinnis's double life. Barbara shook her head slowly, her mind jumping back and forth between events that had happened long ago and the incident at the Wayne Enterprises complex the night before.

A knock came on her office door. "Go away," she yelled, without taking her eyes off the screen.

Terry opened the door and stuck his head into the office. "Morning, Commish," he beamed, flashing his usually irresistible smile. Without waiting for a reply he stepped into the room, closing the door behind him. His backpack was slung over one shoulder, his brown jacket unbuttoned as usual. He dropped his backpack to the floor and took a seat across from the commissioner.

"Don't you understand English, McGinnis?" Barbara asked, pointing to the door. "Scram."

"Love to, I'm late for school anyway," Terry said. "But first, what can you tell me about clowns?"

Barbara turned away from the monitor and looked right at Terry. "In this town they're never funny," she said, the seriousness in her voice unmistakable.

Terry nodded. "I noticed that. Now this Joker character "

"Drop it, kid," Barbara cut him off, not making any attempt to hide the sternness in her warning.

"That's what the old man's been saying," Terry said.

"You should listen to him," Barbara advised. "He usually knows what he's talking about. And in this case . . ." She let the thought hang in the air.

"Look, I know this fruitcake was one of the big bad guys from the old cape-and-cowl days," Terry began.

"He was more than that," Barbara countered. "Much more."

Terry grinned broadly, imitating the man he had confronted the night before. "What? A garden-variety wacko who threatened people with whoopee cushions and squirting flowers? Big deal, I'm shaking!"

"McGinnis!" Barbara shouted, slamming her fist onto the desk. Composing herself, she continued. "The Joker, the *real* Joker, was unlike anyone you've ever faced. For your sake, I hope you never do. If Bruce wants you to drop it, then you should drop it."

Before Terry could utter a response, the phone on Barbara's desk buzzed. "Commissioner, your nine o'clock is here," said a voice from the speaker.

"Send him in," Barbara replied, then turned back to Terry. "You were leaving?"

"I guess I was," he answered, grabbing his backpack and heading for the door.

Terry pulled the door open, and in walked a heavyset man in his mid-fifties. His suit was wrinkled and his eyes were tired and bloodshot, as if he hadn't slept much the night before.

As Terry left the office he overheard the man say, "Thanks for seeing me, Barb."

The commissioner smiled warmly and gestured to a chair. "That's what I'm here for," she replied. "It's good to see you, Tim."

There were times during Bruce Wayne's life when the Batcave felt like a big, lonely place. Often, he sought out the solitude the cave offered, comforted by the quiet emptiness of the huge underground cavern. But tonight, as he sat in front of the Batcomputer with Ace stretched out at his feet, the cave was occupied by more than just the swarm of bats that fluttered among the jagged outcroppings of the ceiling. Tonight the old place was filled with ghosts.

Bruce stared at the computer's enormous monitor. The screen was filled with images of the Joker, mostly from the days when Bruce had battled him as Batman. One picture showed him in full costume — purple coat and gloves, white face, green hair — grinning maniacally. Another showed him in a straitjacket, being monitored by the guards at Arkham Asylum, the hospital for the criminally insane. He had been confined there many times over the years, only to escape or return to criminal ways upon release.

One image showed the man who had disrupted the ceremony the night before. Bruce typed commands into the computer. The picture of the Joker in full costume filled half the screen, the shot from the night before took up the other half. Beneath each photo ran a straight line. Bruce typed some more and then the words VOICE ID appeared on the screen.

The Joker's voice boomed from the computer's speakers: ". . . a countdown of victims that will end at midnight, unless our dear Dark Knight stops me first! Ha-ha-ha-ha!" The line beneath the old Joker photo moved in a jagged pattern along with the voice.

Then a second voice, recorded the night before, rang out. "Hello, Gotham! The Joker's back in town! Ha-ha-ha-ha!" The line under the second photo moved in the same jagged pattern. Bruce hit another key. The words VOICE MATCH IDENTICAL popped up beneath the two jagged lines.

Identical! Bruce thought. *Voice matches don't lie. But it's still impossible. There is no way that man can be the Joker!*

Ace barked once and jumped to his feet, announcing Terry's arrival. A moment later the teenager had stepped up behind Bruce, his backpack slung over his shoulder.

"It's funny," Terry began, looking up at the photos and voice test on the screen. "I know about all your other major enemies, but you never mention him. He was the biggest, wasn't he?"

"It wasn't a popularity contest," Bruce replied, standing up. "He was a psychopath. A monster."

"So how is it possible he could still be around after all this time?" Terry asked.

"It's not possible," Bruce stated flatly. "He died years ago."

"You're sure?" Terry questioned.

Bruce walked into a dark corner of the cave. "I'm sure. I was there."

Terry stared into the shadows for a moment, then spoke softly. "You killed him, didn't you?"

Bruce turned to face his young protégé from the darkness.

"He was going to do something so terrible you had no other choice but to kill him," Terry continued.

"Terry, please," Bruce pleaded.

"That was it, wasn't it?" Terry asked, confident he had hit upon the truth.

Bruce stepped back into the light and walked right up to Terry. In his most serious voice he said, "I want you to give back the Batman suit."

Terry looked at his mentor, stunned. He hadn't expected this, not in his wildest dreams, and he instinctively clutched his backpack. "What?" he said in shock. "Why?"

"There is no reason for you to continue," Bruce stated gently, but firmly. "You've made your father's killers pay for his murder, then put your own needs aside to help the city when it most needed a hero. You've honored the reputation of Batman many times over, and for that I thank you."

"Then why ask for it back?" Terry asked, still stunned by the request.

Bruce walked away from Terry. He looked at the long case displaying the various Batman and Robin costumes, then lowered his eyes. He thought of Dick Grayson, the first Robin, and how he took the orphan in and trained him to be Batman's crime-fighting partner. Then he thought of Tim Drake, the second youngster he had trained to be Robin, and how neither of these young lives turned out quite as he had planned. "I had no right to force this life on you," he said calmly, pausing before he added, "or anyone else."

"Hey, I was the one who broke in and swiped the suit, remember?" Terry reminded Bruce, following close behind him. "That first time was because of my dad's murder. But since then, wearing that suit has come to mean a lot to me. We're from two different worlds, Mr. Wayne. I wasn't like you or the others you took in."

Terry looked away, fighting the embarrassment that washed over him. He had never spoken this honestly about his past to anyone. But he had never had quite so much on the line before. Bruce looked back at him, and Terry took this as a signal to continue.

"I was a pretty bad kid once," Terry admitted. "Ran with a rough crowd, broke a lot of laws, not to mention my folks' hearts. I was the kind of punk you wouldn't have wasted a second punch on, back in your day."

Bruce was growing impatient with Terry's little journey down memory lane. "Your point?" he asked gruffly.

"I'm doing this to make up for past mistakes," Terry blurted out, holding nothing back now. "The state says my slate is clean after serving my three months in juvenile detention, but my soul tells me different. You've never had to look into the eyes of a girlfriend's father and know that no matter what I accomplished in school, all he saw was a 'bad kid,' a kid who 'did time.'

"Every time I put on that suit it's my chance to help people in trouble. Kids who are just as scared and stupid as I was, and about to make the same mistakes. It's being Batman that makes me feel worthwhile again — in my eyes, if no one else's."

Terry looked at Bruce, holding his ground more forcefully than he ever had with his mentor. He respected Bruce tremendously, valued his opinion. But there was no doubt about how he felt when it came to being Batman. "It's my choice. It's what I want, Bruce."

Bruce Wayne scowled and turned away. "Stupid kid," he spat out, anger and frustration in his voice. "You don't know what you want." Walking away, he added, "None of you ever did."

Terry was stunned. He had just poured his heart out only to be rejected outright. His shock turned to anger, his expression souring. Without speaking, he slipped the backpack off his shoulder and slammed it to the ground. Then he turned and stormed up the stairs, out of the Batcave, and away from Wayne Manor.

The backpack flopped open, spilling its contents. The black Batsuit came to rest on the floor of the Batcave. Ace looked up curiously at Bruce, who was staring down at the Batsuit, lost in his own thoughts.

CHAPTER SIX

The modest house that Terry shared with his mother and eight-year-old brother, Matt, was flooded with sunlight the following morning. Terry stumbled down the stairs in his bathrobe and fixed himself a bowl of cold cereal. He flopped into a chair at the kitchen table and was pouring some milk into his bowl when Matt skidded into the room, stopping abruptly. He stared at his big brother, eyes wide, mouth gaping open.

"Mom! Come quick!" Matt shouted. "Some weirdo broke into our house and he's eating all our cereal!"

Terry ignored his brother and continued to shovel spoonfuls of cereal into his mouth.

"Matty?" his mom called from upstairs. "What are you yelling about?"

"There's a stranger sitting at our kitchen table!" Matt shouted back.

"Ha-ha," Terry said through a mouthful of cereal.

Mary McGinnis came into the kitchen and sat next to her eldest son. "That's your brother, Matt," she said, playing along.

"Never seen the dreg before in my life," Matt replied with a laugh, pouring some cereal for himself.

"It *is* unusual for you to be around here, Terry," Mary said, sensing something was wrong. "And it's rare that you're up and about before noon, what with you working late for Mr. Wayne and all."

Terry stared into his cereal bowl. Mary placed a comforting hand on his shoulder. She realized that he wasn't ready to talk about whatever was troubling him. She had learned to give her son lots of space and leeway since his father's death. Terry appreciated her for it.

"Well, it's nice to have you home for a change," Mary said, smiling. "Right, Matt?"

"Sure, great," Matt replied sarcastically. "Just when I was getting used to being an only child!"

Using his spoon as a slingshot, Terry fired a piece of cereal at his brother. It hit Matt right on the nose.

"Mom!" Matt whined.

Mary shook her head and got up from the table. "Boys," she sighed.

Bruce Wayne stepped from the elevator out onto the terrace of the Wayne Enterprises complex. The place was still a wreck, looking very much as it had after the Joker's attack. As Bruce surveyed the damage, Jordan Pryce supervised the cleanup team.

"Clear the garbage away and sweep up that glass," he ordered, gesturing at the mess all around him.

"Yes, sir," replied a uniformed worker.

Pryce spotted Bruce and walked over to join him. "Well, Bruce, looks like your return party brought out the lunatic fringe in full force."

"They weren't on my guest list," Bruce replied dryly. "Sorry I missed you at the party."

"It was your night," Pryce explained, heading toward his office. "I didn't want to be in the way."

Bruce followed Pryce, stopping at the door to his office. "Jordan," he began, "I know you're not happy with my return."

Pryce looked right at Bruce. "Please," he said, holding up his hand. "I'm not paid to have an opinion on the matter. You are the head of this corporation, and I will strive to do the best for the company, as any good employee would." Then he gave Bruce an odd look. "Hmm."

"Something wrong?" Bruce asked.

"No," Pryce replied. "It's just I noticed that you're alone today. Usually you have Terry to assist you."

"I'm surprised someone in your position would remember the name of a boy you'd seen maybe once before," Bruce stated. He was impressed by Pryce's sharp mind, but suspicious about his reason for recalling Terry's name.

Pryce gestured to his office. Bruce followed him inside. The room was a model of success, achievement, and luxury. A sleek, modern desk lined one whole side of the office. A wall-sized window offered a spectacular view of Gotham. Wooden bookcases lined the remaining walls. Plush couches and chairs were available for visitors, and Bruce settled into a large, overstuffed chair.

"I got to my position by being thorough, Bruce," Pryce explained as he poured himself a drink. "Besides, I've made it a point to know everything there is to know about the man I work for."

Bruce looked at him curiously.

"I've done my research," Pryce explained. "You were orphaned at age eight and educated abroad. You returned to Gotham fifteen years later, but for more than two decades only took a passing interest in day-to-day company operations. Seems you developed somewhat of a playboy reputation, late hours, nightly carousing — at least, according to rumors."

Bruce shrugged. "The foolishness of youth."

"Still," Pryce continued, "during that time you charitably served as legal guardian to two orphaned boys. And later you were publicly linked to now – Police Commissioner Barbara Gordon, though you never married."

Bruce laughed softly. "Hardly the stuff of legends."

"Maybe not," Pryce went on, toasting Bruce with his glass. "But, like I said, I *am* thorough."

The phone on Pryce's desk beeped. "Mr. Pryce?" came his secretary's voice. "Your lunch appointment is waiting."

"On my way," Pryce replied into the speakerphone. Then turning to Bruce he asked, "You'll be okay here on your own?"

"You would know," Bruce replied, managing a tiny smile.

"Yes," Pryce said, returning the smile, "I would." Then he left the office, with Bruce staring suspiciously after him.

The last light of the afternoon was fading fast. Rain fell gently from a slate-gray sky as Bruce Wayne's limo negotiated the twists and turns of a narrow country road on the outskirts of Gotham City. Ace, in the passenger seat, cocked his head quizzically and stared at his master, who voiced his thoughts as he drove.

"I'm standing by my decision," Bruce stated firmly. "I was a fool to allow McGinnis to assume the role of Batman. It's no life for anyone, and you can quote me on that!"

In the woods just off the road, Terry McGinnis sat astride his motorcycle, patiently waiting. When Bruce's limo passed the spot where he hid, Terry flipped down the visor on his helmet and slowly pulled out onto the lonely road, keeping far enough back to stay out of sight.

Bruce turned off onto an unpaved lane and started up a steep, winding hill, carefully navigating the ruts and rocks scattered across the long-neglected road. He soon came to the rusted remains of a large iron gate. Beyond sat the ruins of a building. Bruce coasted to a stop just before the gate. A chill slid up his spine to the base of his skull.

"Arkham Asylum," he muttered. Ace growled slightly at the old structure, sensing Bruce's change of mood, and maybe something else. The former psychiatric hospital had been home to some of the most violent, dangerously disturbed criminals the world had ever seen. Now the inmates were housed in newer, more modern facilities. But Bruce believed he could find answers here in the half-rotted remains of a building full of memories and ghosts.

Bruce continued up to the main entrance. He could see that half the building was gone, taken down by work crews who had begun to dismantle the decaying relic. The other half of the asylum looked very much as it had years before, when it was still open.

Ace barked loudly as Bruce stepped out of the car.

"Stay!" Bruce commanded. Ace stopped barking and stretched out on the seat. Bruce cautiously pushed open the asylum's main door and stepped inside.

Terry's motorcycle rolled past the rusty iron gate and slowed to a stop. Leaving his bike around a bend and out of sight of the limo, Terry pulled off his helmet and started up to the ruin on foot. As he passed the limo, Ace perked up, barking and wagging his tail.

Terry gestured for the dog to be quiet. "Shhh! Yeah, I'm happy to see you, too. But I need you to be quiet now. Can't let the old man know I'm following him." Terry carefully stepped through the open entryway, moving slowly, keeping as close to Bruce as possible while remaining unseen.

Bruce Wayne strode through the dark building, scanning its many hallways and rooms. He came to a row of long-abandoned jail cells, many of which still had hand-written signs bearing the names of the last occupant. Bruce read DENT, H. on a cell in which half the padding had been torn off the walls. *Two-Face*, he thought. ISLEY, P. was above a cell whose floor was covered in dead leaves. *Poison Ivy*. The walls of the last cell he passed were covered in faded, crudely drawn question marks. NYGMA, E. the sign read. *The Riddler*, Bruce thought, shaking his head and shuddering. *Too many bad memories*.

Slowly he moved past a barrier set up by the demolition crew. It blocked off the half of the building that had mostly been removed. Here the structure was open to the outside, and Bruce heard the sound of a nearby stream. He continued down the hall until he came to a large pair of double doors. Painted in flaking gold letters on the glass in the center of each door were the words OPERATING THEATER. Bruce took a deep breath, then pushed the doors open and stepped inside.

It took a few minutes for his eyes to adjust to the dim light. A row of primitive-looking operating tables lined the lowest level of the theater. Above, a row of broken, rusted machines sat in a semicircle. Above that sat row after row of observation seats for those who had to watch the grim proceedings below.

Bruce looked up to the ceiling and gasped at what he saw. He caught his breath, grabbed hold of a railing to keep his balance, then turned and fled the room.

Terry quickly crouched down in a corner near the operating theater. Bruce bashed through the double doors, sending them flying wide open. Terry stayed low, out of sight, until Bruce had left the building. Then he stepped into the theater and looked up.

There, suspended in the dim glow of a broken skylight, hung what looked like a man. Taking a closer look, Terry saw that it was a dummy, hung by the neck, spinning in the partial breeze drifting through the broken windows. Terry climbed to the top of the observation level and got a better view.

The crudely formed dummy was made to look like the Joker, complete with white face, green hair, purple suit, and purple gloves. And painted across the body were the mysterious but chilling words:

I KNOW.

CHAPTER SEVEN

The nightly party at Gotham's hottest dance club was well under way when Dana and her friend Chelsea strolled into the club. Lights flashed in rhythm to the beat of the dance mix served up by the club's DJ. Dana and Chelsea had gone all out and dressed in glittering dance outfits. They swayed to the music as they strolled slowly across the dance floor, checking out the crowd.

"Every once in a while we have to ditch the guys and have a night out to ourselves, Dane," Chelsea said as she glided across the room.

"It may be a change for you, Chels," Dana responded, "but I don't see enough of Terry to know the difference."

"Well, Terry's sweet and all," Chelsea admitted, "but who says you can't make friends with someone new?"

"Not a chance," came a familiar voice from behind

Dana. Terry danced up to his girlfriend, took her hand, and the couple shuffled away from Chelsea.

"I thought you'd be working," Dana said, surprise and pleasure showing in her voice.

"Uh-uh," replied Terry, his face turning serious. "The bad news is, for the time being, I'm not going to have much money coming in. I'm no longer working for Mr. Wayne." Terry's face brightened. "The good news is, you have me all to yourself."

Dana smiled. "I can live with that." The two hugged, then continued dancing.

Suddenly, all eyes turned to a corner of the dance floor. A spotlight focused on identical twins in dazzling, skin-tight dance outfits moving together in perfect time to the music. The two girls finished their routine, then strutted across the dance floor. Heads turned to follow the beautiful twins, who were obviously looking to draw attention to themselves — and succeeding.

The twins stepped up to Terry and Dana. One slipped in between the couple, who were busy dancing. "Cutting in," she said, pushing Dana away with a shift of her hips.

"Hey!" Dana cried, stumbling back into the crowd. "What gives? Cutting in is one thing, but this is more like *butting* in!"

"Please excuse my evil twin here," the other girl apologized. "I can't take her anyplace."

"As if!" the first girl squealed, pointing at her sister. "*She's* the bad one!"

Dana started toward the first girl, ready for a fight. But before she could get close, a large gangly man wearing clown makeup stepped out from behind a large bank of speakers. He grabbed Dana, covering her mouth to stifle her gasp. Then he pulled her into the shadows.

The second twin had distracted Terry long enough for him to have missed Dana's abduction. "Dana?" he called out, looking around. Swiftly the twins each grabbed one of Terry's arms and steered him into the thick, gyrating crowd.

"Excuse me," Terry said, yanking his arms free and pushing back through the crowd. "Dana!" he shouted, scanning the dance floor.

Terry caught a flash of motion out of the corner of his eye, but he was too late. He picked up the spinning form of one of the twins just as she kicked him in the jaw, sending him sprawling into the throng of dancers. "Hey!" he cried in shock.

"It was her," the twin who had kicked him said. She smiled innocently and pointed to her sister.

Terry continued looking for Dana, moving away from

the twins. They followed and again each grabbed an arm. This time they pulled him back roughly.

"Don't run away," the first girl said.

"All the boys love us!" the second one cackled.

Then they spoke together. "We're trouble on the double!"

In a flash, Terry realized he was dealing with the Dee-Dee twins from the Jokerz gang. He quickly grabbed each girl's head and banged them together.

"Ow!" they cried in unison.

Terry heard a growl from behind him. He spun around in time to see Woof leap high over the dancing crowd. There was no time to react. Woof landed right on top of him. The two tumbled backward, crashing hard through a table and slamming to the ground. The crowd of horrified dancers screamed and ran for the exits.

Woof jumped off Terry and circled for another attack. Terry instinctively flipped his wrist, hoping to summon a Batarang. Then he grimaced at his foolishness. His costume was back at the Batcave.

Woof leapt again, but this time Terry was prepared. He rolled onto his back and kicked the half-human beast away. Woof went flying into a nearby speaker. Electric sparks crackled through the dust.

But there wasn't even a second to recover. One Dee-

Dee grabbed Terry from behind, while the other Dee-Dee launched herself, feetfirst, at his midsection. She landed a sharp, two-footed kick to his gut. Terry collapsed, just in time for Chucko to join the party. He grabbed Terry by the hair and yanked his head back.

"I dunno why the boss wants a loser like you out of the way, but hey, as long as it's fun." Chucko grinned. Then he slammed into Terry with his best right hook, sending him sprawling to the floor.

Not far away, Dana struggled furiously to free herself from Ghoul's grasp. She brought her sharp heel down onto the top of Ghoul's foot. As he yelped in pain, she broke free and ran. "Terry!" she shouted, scrambling to get away.

But Ghoul was quick. He reached out and grabbed Dana, pulling her back.

Terry heard his name and looked up in time to see Ghoul grabbing Dana roughly. He jumped to his feet and raced toward them. Chucko stepped into his path, but Terry was so enraged at the thought of the Jokerz harming Dana, he brushed the gang member aside. The Dee-Dees came after Terry next, but he swiftly vaulted over them, knocking their heads together again for good measure.

Meanwhile, Ghoul had grown impatient with Dana's struggling. He dragged her to the edge of a platform high up on the club's top level and shoved her off.

Terry spotted his girlfriend's situation as he raced through the quickly emptying club. "Dana! No!" he shouted. Timing his leap, he caught her falling body before it reached the floor. The impact sent him crashing into a nearby table. He quickly scrambled to his knees and looked into her eyes. "Wake up, Dana," he cried. "You've got to be okay!"

Nearby, Chucko was tossing blasters to the Dee-Dees. He kept one for himself. The Jokerz opened fire, sending the remaining dancers diving for cover behind overturned tables.

Terry dashed through the club with Dana in his arms, shielding her body with his. He spotted Chelsea, who was crouched in terror behind the juice bar. "Stay here and watch Dana," he told her. "I've got to stop those guys so we can get her out of here and to a hospital."

Chelsea nodded and pulled Dana's limp body close to her, wondering exactly what Terry planned to do against a gang of crazed clowns carrying blasters.

Terry wondered the same thing himself. Then he spotted the club's giant slushie machine. The thirty-foot-tall glass machine was used to dispense frozen juice drinks to the club's patrons. But Terry had other plans for it.

He dashed up the stairs to the same high platform Dana had been pushed from. Darting left and then right, he kept low, dodging streams of blaster fire from the gang below. Then, taking a running start, Terry leapt from the platform. He landed on top of the slushie machine.

"What's he doing?" Dee-Dee asked, watching Terry climb around to the far side of the machine.

"Maybe he's thirsty," the other Dee-Dee suggested, laughing.

"Just finish him!" Chucko ordered, firing another blast.

Terry scooted to the rear of the machine. Bracing his back against the wall, he pushed the top of the machine with his feet. It started rocking back and forth. Using the momentum, Terry rocked it again, then a third time, kicking out with his legs. The huge glass tower toppled forward. Terry slid down its side, riding the glass like a snowboarder on the slopes. He jumped off just as the machine hit the floor.

CRASSSHH!

The massive container shattered, sending thousands of gallons of sticky, icy slush across the dance floor like a tidal wave.

Chucko caught up to Terry as the sloshing liquid rolled up over his ankles. "Aww, you made a mess, dreg," he said sarcastically, aiming his blaster right at Terry's chest. He pulled the trigger, but instead of deadly laser fire, blue-green slush belched from his blaster.

Chucko stared down at his weapon — and never even saw Terry's punch coming. Terry flattened the chunky clown just as the slushie wave hit the club's lighting generator. Sparks flew as the liquid seeped into the high-voltage box.

THOOOM!

The generator exploded, plunging the room into darkness. Flames burst out and small explosions ripped through the club. The Jokerz raced toward the back door through the flaming chaos. Their mission to get rid of Terry was a failure.

Terry, meanwhile, dashed back to the bar. Chelsea and Dana were gone. The frantic teenager ran outside in time to see Dana being strapped onto a waiting ambulance gurney.

"She's got a bad bump and some cuts but she's going to be okay," Chelsea explained to Terry as the paramedics loaded Dana into the ambulance. "Why were those guys after you?"

"I don't know," Terry replied, head down. Then he grasped Chelsea by the shoulders. "Look, I'm going to go talk to the cops. Stay with Dana, okay, Chels? I'll come as soon as I can."

"Sure," Chelsea said, climbing into the back of the ambulance.

Terry watched as the ambulance pulled away. He could only think of how he was to blame for putting his girlfriend's life in danger. But he couldn't let that stop him. He ran toward his motorcycle, trying to make sense of what had just happened.

CHAPTER EIGHT

Deep in the Batcave, Bruce Wayne was hard at work mixing chemicals at a lab table. Ace slept by his feet. Several different mixtures sat in rounded vials on the table. A large beaker warmed on a burner, smoke rising from the liquid's surface. One small vial was labeled JOKER ANTITOXIN.

Ace jumped to his feet, letting out a low, menacing growl. "What is it, boy?" Bruce asked. Ace's tail whipped back and forth, his teeth bared. Then the hound rushed forward, bolting up the stairs to the Wayne Manor library. "Ace!" Bruce shouted after him.

Bruce could hear Ace's savage growls and barking. It sounded as if a struggle was going on, as if Ace was attacking someone or something. Then there was a high-pitched yelp, followed by silence.

"Ace!" Bruce shouted, leaping to his feet and grabbing his cane. He started for the stairs, then stopped suddenly at the sight of a round, ball-like object bouncing down toward him. Bruce instinctively backed away as the object stopped at the bottom of the stairs. He had just a moment to glimpse a smiley face painted onto the round metal globe before it exploded, releasing a cloud of gas.

Bruce covered his mouth, coughing and gasping for breath. He staggered to the lab table and grasped at several vials of the antitoxin he'd been working on. The slender glass vials tumbled from his trembling hands. One shattered, another rolled under the table.

On his knees and choking now, Bruce stared up through tearing eyes to see a tall silhouette slowly descending the stairs. As the figure grew closer, Bruce recognized him. It was the Joker.

"Don't get up, Bruce," he cackled. "It's just an old friend come by to say hello."

Bruce struggled to get to his feet, but the Joker moved swiftly, grabbing him by his jacket and knocking him back into a chair. He forced his hateful, grinning face close to Bruce's. "Hello, Batman," he spat out, laughing uncontrollably at his long-awaited moment of triumph. Then he lunged for Bruce's neck.

Terry's motorcycle wove its way through the Gotham City traffic, ducking between trucks and around cars. Terry pressed a control switch on his helmet and the built-in cell phone dialed the number at Wayne Manor.

"Leave a message," came Bruce Wayne's terse voice.

Terry spoke quickly after the beep. "Hey! The Joker's little playmates came after *me* tonight. Me, not Batman. This whole thing stinks, Wayne, and you know why. I need some straight answers from —" Terry suddenly realized that something was wrong. "It's night," he muttered to himself. "He never goes out at night. Why isn't he picking up?" He disconnected the call and gunned the bike's engine, tearing down the avenue.

A few minutes later, Terry roared through the entrance to Wayne Manor, growing more disturbed at the sight of the unlocked gate. Leaping from his bike, he raced through the open front door.

"Wayne?" Terry called out. "Wayne?" he yelled again, entering the library. A weak whimper stopped him in his tracks. Ace was stretched out in a corner, struggling to wake up. Terry knelt beside the dazed dog and stroked his head gently. Then he glanced at the large grandfather clock that served as the secret entrance to the Batcave. It had been shoved to one side, and the stairway to

Bruce Wayne's secret lair stood open, exposed and vulnerable.

Dashing down the stairs, Terry gasped at the sight of spray-painted words — HA! HA! HA! HA! — that covered everything. The walls and floor of the Batcave were covered with the Joker's signature graffiti. So were the many artifacts and souvenirs of Batman's illustrious past. The long display case of costumes was shattered. The dummies wearing the Batman, Nightwing, and Batgirl costumes were knocked over, scattered on the floor. The Robin costume had been torn to shreds.

"Please, no!" Terry whispered, scanning the Batcave. Then he spotted Bruce slumped over the Batcomputer. Terry rushed to his side and gently turned him over. The sight of his mentor made his heart stop cold. The Joker's hideous grin spread across Bruce's face like a horrible mask. His eyes appeared lifeless.

Panic swept through Terry. He grabbed Bruce, stretched him out on the floor and furiously pumped his chest. "Come on, move!" he cried.

Bruce's parched lips parted slightly and a terrible, unnatural giggle came out. Terry was horrified and confused, but relieved that at least Bruce was alive. Fighting to speak through giggles he seemed unable to control, Bruce gasped out a few words. "Floor . . . under . . . table," he wheezed.

Terry dashed to the table and dropped to his knees, grabbing the vial of Joker antitoxin that Bruce had dropped earlier. He quickly loaded it into a spray hypo and injected the serum into Bruce's arm.

Instantly, Bruce's features softened and the masklike grin dissolved into a tired, sober look. Bruce's head relaxed, then fell to one side, and he drifted off into a fitful sleep. Terry ran to the phone and called the only person he could think of for help. Then he slung Bruce over his shoulder and carried him upstairs.

A short while later, Barbara Gordon arrived at Wayne Manor. She went to Bruce's bedside, looking down at the man who had played such a huge role in her life. First in her days as Batgirl to his Batman, then in her personal relationship with Bruce, she became one of the few people he had ever allowed to get close to him. She had reluctantly continued their collaboration once she became Gotham's police commissioner.

Barbara dabbed at his fevered brow with a damp cloth, then kissed him gently on the forehead.

"How is he?" Terry asked, entering the bedroom.

"The antitoxin's done all it can," Barbara explained. "It's up to him now."

"Thanks for coming," Terry offered. "I didn't know who else to call."

Barbara smiled knowingly and shrugged. "Who else is there?"

"That reminds me," Terry said. "I'd better check on our other patient."

Terry headed downstairs to the living room, where Ace was sprawled out on the couch, watching TV. "How you doing, killer?" he asked playfully, scratching Ace's huge head. "Yeah, rough night for me, too." He grabbed the TV remote and hit the news channel. The computer-generated newsman was smiling as usual. But it was the picture of Bruce in the upper right-hand corner of the screen that caused Terry to snap to attention.

"Sad news from the financial world this morning," the anchor began. "The return of Bruce Wayne to his family's company has been delayed due to an accident. Jordan Pryce, of Wayne Enterprises, had this to say."

"We received a call from Mr. Wayne's houseboy this morning saying Mr. Wayne had taken a bad fall," Pryce explained, his image replacing Bruce's.

"Houseboy!" Terry cried indignantly as Barbara entered the room.

"I will be filling in for Mr. Wayne during his extended convalescence. Everyone here at Wayne Enterprises sends their good wishes for a speedy recovery. . . ."

"I'll bet," Terry muttered, flipping off the TV. He looked

at Barbara. "Obviously, not every creep in Gotham wears a purple suit."

"It'd make my job simpler if they did," the commissioner replied.

"The Joker knew about Bruce, about me, probably about you, too," Terry said.

"Someone knows," Barbara admitted. "I'll give you that. But he's not the Joker. Not the real one."

"Bruce said he was dead," Terry told Barbara.

"And . . . ?" Barbara asked.

"That's all I know," Terry said. "But I also know there's more. Barbara, I'm a part of this. I need the answers Bruce can't give me now. I deserve them."

Barbara lowered her eyes in resignation. She knew Terry was right. She had to tell him the whole horrible story. "I thought talking about it would get easier over time, but some memories never go away."

As she stared out the window at the Gotham skyline, Barbara's mind raced back to another Gotham — the Gotham of the days when she fought crime as Batgirl, with Batman and Robin at her side.

"It was roughly thirty-five years ago," she began, her eyes fixed on the skyline. "Dick Grayson, the original Robin, had begun to fight crime as Nightwing. He'd left Gotham to establish himself in another city. There were three of us then, Bruce, myself, and the new Robin — Tim Drake."

Terry nodded, listening intently.

"Robin was out alone one night when he came upon a woman in trouble."

CHAPTER NINE

Thirty-five years ago . . .

"Help! Help!" came the terrified screams.

Robin looked down into the alley below the rooftop he'd just landed on. The Boy Wonder fired a Batline and swung down to the alley. Two thugs were closing in on a young woman.

Robin slammed into the attackers feetfirst, knocking them to the ground. Then he did a midair flip and landed in front of the woman. "That evens things up a bit," the young crime fighter said.

"Not really, bird-boy," the woman replied.

Robin recognized the voice instantly. "Harley!" he cried. Harley Quinn was the Joker's partner and his girlfriend of sorts. Robin realized immediately that he had just swung into a trap.

Harley pulled a mallet from her coat. "Now just hold still and this won't hurt a bit!" she said, whacking Robin on the head.

The two thugs leapt at Robin. Battling through the pain in his head, Robin fought back. Harley raised the mallet for another blow, but Robin yanked it from her hand, sending her flying into a row of garbage cans.

That's when a purple-gloved hand grabbed the teenager by the shoulder and shocked him with a massive charge of electricity.

"Arrrrgg!" Robin cried, falling to the ground, knocked unconscious.

A maniacal laugh echoed through the alley as the Joker stepped out of the shadows. "You know what they say about a bird in the hand," he cackled, smoke still rising from his electric joy buzzer.

The thugs dragged Robin from the alley as Harley hugged the grinning Joker. Then the happy twosome followed their hired lackeys and took Robin back to their secret lair.

It didn't take long for Batman and Batgirl to realize that Robin was missing. Night after night they scoured the city, searching everywhere, interrogating criminals, tracking down even the tiniest lead. For three agonizing weeks they looked — but they found no sign of Tim.

Then, one night, an invitation arrived. Following its instructions, Batman and Batgirl swooped down to the roof of an abandoned warehouse. A huge, brightly colored package that looked like a giant jack-in-the-box greeted them.

Batman cautiously tossed a Batarang at the box's latch, popping it open, and a dummy of Robin sprang from the box. It was dressed in a straitjacket.

Suddenly, the dummy's head popped off. Batman instinctively pulled Batgirl to safety behind a chimney, just as the rolling head exploded. The blast sent a shower of smoke and confetti spraying all around them. When the smoke had cleared, Batman looked at the charred remains of the dummy. On the still smoldering straitjacket a single word was written.

"Arkham," Batman muttered, scowling.

Arkham Asylum had been abandoned for a while. The inmates had been moved to a newer, high-security building, while the old facility had been partially demolished and left to the elements.

The Batmobile bashed through the locked gate of the old asylum. It screeched to a stop, and Batman and Batgirl leapt from their seats and dashed up the rickety front steps. The two heroes cautiously made their way inside.

The sound of a woman's voice singing a soft lullaby led them through the mazelike corridors to the asylum's operating theater. Stepping through the double doors, Batman and Batgirl were greeted by a bizarre sight. The huge room had been decorated to look like a twisted version of a normal home. Furniture and large toys were strewn all around. Areas of the enormous loft had been partitioned off with makeshift walls to form rooms.

Batgirl quietly slipped away, climbing to the highest level of the theater. Batman, meanwhile, stepped to the center of the main level in time to see Harley Quinn lovingly place a vase of flowers onto a table. "Puddin'!" she called out. "Company!"

The Joker slowly descended a long stairway. "Hello there!" he sang out. "Welcome to our happy home!"

"Where's Robin?" Batman demanded, in no mood for joking around.

Harley and the Joker looked at each other and shrugged. "Robin?" the Joker replied. "There's no Robin here."

"Maybe he means our little Jay," Harley suggested.

"Why, of course," the Joker chirped, snapping his fingers. "That's it!"

From behind a curtained-off area, the sound of a boy's hysterical laughter echoed through the room. Shoving

Harley aside, Batman strode purposefully toward the curtain. As if on cue, Harley pulled a strange-looking, clownish bazooka from under a table and fired it. Brightly colored streamers shot from the weapon's muzzle, pinning one of Batman's arms to his side.

Up at the top of the room, Batgirl pulled out her grappling gun, ready to swoop down. But Batman subtly signaled her to stay put and remain ready.

"Y'know, Bats," the Joker began. "We've been doing this little runaround of ours for years. It's been loads of fun, but the fact is, none of us is getting any younger. And so Harley and I were thinking that it was time we settled down and started a family. We decided to adopt. It would have been hard for us to do it legally, but then we remembered you always have a few spare kids hanging around."

The Joker whipped open the curtains that had been dividing the room. "So we borrowed one of yours."

Batman and Batgirl both gasped at the sight revealed by the parting curtains. Robin was strapped to a medical table in the center of the room. His face was painted white, his hair was dyed green, and he was wearing a suit just like the Joker's.

The Joker and Harley stood behind Robin, beaming down at him like proud parents. "He needed a little molding, of course," the Joker announced. "But what kid doesn't? After a little bit of time, we came to love him as our own. Say hello, son."

Robin turned to Batman with a blank stare, giggling insanely.

Rage welled up within Batman's chest. He instinctively started toward Robin. But the Joker activated a remote-control device, and the operating table rolled away. Unable to contain herself any longer, Batgirl swung down from above, slamming into Harley. Then she leapt onto the rolling table, leaning in close as she loosened the straps that held her friend. "Robin!" she shouted.

Robin giggled wildly.

"Tim," Batgirl whispered. "It's Barbara. Can you hear me?"

Robin shook his head, shouting, "No, no, no!" He pushed Batgirl away and leapt from the table.

Harley grabbed Batgirl from behind. The two struggled, tumbling through the theater's double doors, rolling to the edge of the building. The two women grappled as rain poured down on the half-demolished structure. Alongside them was a broken ledge that dropped off many stories to the street below.

Batgirl flipped Harley over and pinned her on her back. "How could you help the Joker do it, Harley?"

"So we roughed the kid up a bit," Harley replied, kicking Batgirl off her. "But soon we'll be one big happy family."

And with that, Robin stepped from the shadows, holding the clownish bazooka.

"Good boy," Harley cooed. "Now give it to Mama!"

"Robin, no!" Batgirl shouted, but it was too late. Robin tossed the bazooka to Harley, who trained the bizarre weapon on her.

Without hesitation Harley fired. Colored streamers headed right for Batgirl's legs, but she leapt up and the streamers zoomed by beneath her feet. They struck the barricade right in front of the ledge as Batgirl somersaulted forward and landed in front of Harley, knocking the weapon from her hands.

The bazooka landed at Harley's feet and went off. Streamers wrapped around her legs and knocked her through the barricade. Batgirl reached out and grabbed Harley's arm to stop her fall, but both women dropped over the ledge. With her free hand, Batgirl grabbed an outcropping and managed to stop her fall. But Harley lost her grip and plunged into the darkness below.

Meanwhile, Batman was tearing through the theater, searching for the Joker. "What's the matter, Batman?" the Joker taunted, his voice seeming to come from everywhere at once. "No witty comebacks? No scary threats? Then I guess I'll just have to provide the narration."

The lights abruptly went out, and a grainy home movie

flickered on a side wall of the theater. Images of Robin being subjected to the Joker's demented villainy flashed across the screen. Batman was speechless with horror.

"You would have been proud to see him so strong," the Joker went on. "But eventually the dear lad broke down and began to share secrets with me. Secrets that are now mine alone to know . . . Bruce."

A silhouette of the Joker's face appeared on the screen, blocking out the light from the projector. Batman watched as the Joker popped a candy into his mouth, then continued his taunts. "It's true, Batsy. I know everything. You're just a little boy in a playsuit, crying for Mommy and Daddy. It'd be funny if it wasn't so pathetic." The Joker shrugged. "Oh, what the heck. I'll laugh anyway! *HA-HA-H —*"

CRASH!!

The Joker's shrill laughter was cut short. Batman had crashed through the projection booth window. The Dark Knight smashed into the Joker, who crumpled to the floor like a rag doll whose seams had come undone. Batman grabbed him and tossed him through the broken window onto the theater's floor. "I'm finishing this now, Joker," Batman snarled, his rage boiling over.

"Oh, Batman," the Joker sneered. "If you had any guts, you would have finished it years ago. I, on the other hand . . ." The Joker subtly moved a knife hidden in his sleeve into his waiting hand. He slashed right through the bat symbol on Batman's chest, then brought the knife down across Batman's leg.

The Caped Crusader fell to the floor in pain, clutching his leg.

"You've lost, Batman," the Joker snarled, casting the knife aside. "Robin is mine." He tossed Robin a brightly colored dart shooter that looked like a child's toy. "Here you go, sonny-boy, make Daddy proud," the Joker cackled. "You deliver the punch line."

Robin grinned insanely and grasped the weapon with both hands. Giggling wildly, he looked from the Joker to Batman.

Batman looked up at Robin. The heartbreak of what had become of his young friend overwhelmed any fear he felt. "Tim," he called out softly. "Don't do this, Tim."

"Do it!" the Joker ordered, his face a twisted, grinning mask of rage.

Robin's hands shook. The unnatural smile that had been frozen on his face melted into a look of panic and confusion. He giggled faster now, more afraid. Then he pointed the dart shooter at Batman, hesitated, and fired. But as he did so, he turned. A thin dart flew from the weapon. A small flag that said BANG! unfurled from the dart and wedged in the Joker's chest.

The Joker looked down in disbelief. "That's not funny," he muttered, starting to fall forward. His smile faded. "That's not funny at all." Then he collapsed, motionless.

Robin dropped the weapon. His forced giggling turned into heaving sobs. Batman struggled to drag himself over to his distraught partner.

Batgirl got there first. She hugged Robin tightly. "It's okay, Tim," she said comfortingly. "It's over. You're coming home with us."

CHAPTER TEN

Terry McGinnis sat on a couch in Bruce Wayne's living room, completely caught up in the incredible account he had just heard.

Barbara Gordon was still staring out the window as she finished her story. "We buried the Joker deep beneath Arkham. The only other person who knew what happened that night was my father, James, the first Commissioner Gordon. He promised to keep our secret. With his last act of cruelty, the Joker had tainted us all with compromise and deception." She took off her glasses and rubbed her weary eyes. Reliving these events had drained her of energy, not to mention hope. "I suppose, in some ways, the Joker had the last laugh after all."

Terry was overwhelmed. A number of things had

become clear to him as he listened to the terrible tale. "I'm assuming Harley Quinn bought it that night, too," he said, trying to fit all the pieces together.

"We never found her body," Barbara responded. "But I doubt she'd be starting trouble now."

"And Drake?" Terry asked, a little afraid of the answer he might receive.

"It took a year of hard work with an excellent doctor, but Tim Drake eventually regained his sanity," Barbara replied. "Still, things were never the same. Bruce . . . Batman . . . forbade Tim to be Robin again. He blamed himself for what had happened and swore he'd never endanger another young partner again. But Tim disagreed. He felt he had earned the right to make that choice for himself."

Terry smiled in recognition. "I can relate."

"Tim left us soon after that," Barbara continued. "He was determined to make it on his own."

"Did they ever patch things up?" Terry asked.

Barbara shook her head sadly. "Not really. Tim tried once or twice, but you know Bruce. I check up on Tim now and then. In fact, that was him you saw in my office the other day. He's a top-level communications engineer now. Married, a couple of kids. Not too bad, all things considered."

Terry nodded, his mind racing. "He deserves a happy

ending. But as far as our little mystery goes, Tim Drake still has the most likely connection to that night . . . and to the Joker."

Gotham City's huge communications tower rose above most of the other structures in town. The tall, needlelike building reached high into the sky, beaming audio, video, and data signals for hundred of miles in all directions.

As an evening chill engulfed Gotham, a uniformed man in a hover-bucket glided to a spot just below the top of the tower. Silently, the man checked some readouts on a flashing piece of electronic equipment attached to the outside of the tower. "It looks okay on this side," he spoke into a wrist communicator. "I'm going up to the dish."

The engineer made his way to the large communications dish that sat like a crown on the very top of the tower. He pulled out his tools and went to work reattaching frayed fiber-optic wires.

A tiny glimmer of movement flashed out of the corner of his eye and a shudder ran up his spine. The quiet, scraping footsteps that followed were unmistakable. "You can turn off the camo mode," he said loudly, not taking his eyes off what he was doing. "I heard you a mile away."

A figure crouching on the dish faded into view — the dark, slender figure of Batman. He had been using the suit to camouflage himself, taking on the appearance of his surroundings — the tiles on the communications dish.

Slowly guiding the hover-bucket through the darkening sky, the engineer was soon face-to-face with Batman. "Tim Drake. I'm no Boy Wonder anymore," the man said, smiling. "But that old training never goes away, even at my age." He nodded at Batman.

Batman returned the gesture. "You heard about Bruce?" he asked.

"Barbara told me," Tim replied, shrugging. "That was too bad."

"You don't seem too broken up about it," Batman observed.

Tim stared the Future Knight directly in the eyes. "I had nothing to do with it, despite what you might be thinking," he declared. "When the Joker reappeared, I was just as surprised as anyone." Tim dropped his head and sighed deeply. "Barb told you the gory details?"

"More or less," Batman replied.

Tim maneuvered his hover-bucket to a control panel just below the dish. Batman scrambled down, following. "Look," Tim began, "it's been thirty-five years. It wasn't easy, but I managed to put it to bed and go on with my life. You'll have to do it yourself one day. We all did. We gave our best, but in the end that wasn't good enough for the old man."

"Regrets, Mr. Drake?" Batman asked.

Tim shook his head slowly, then looked away. "Capes, costumes, playing hero — it was kid stuff. Bruce probably did me a favor. In the end, I was so sick of it I never wanted to see that stupid Robin suit again."

Tim turned around, but Batman was gone, swallowed up by the Gotham night. Tim smirked. "Some things never change." Shaking his head, he went back to work.

The Batmobile streaked toward Gotham Harbor. Batman was talking to Commissioner Gordon, who sat at the Bat-computer's control console in the Batcave. "Were all of you that bitter when you left Bruce?" he asked.

"It comes with the territory, McGinnis," she replied, glancing around the Batcave. Too many memories. "Hunt up Nightwing someday. Has *he* got stories!"

Batman laughed softly. He knew Barbara was referring to Dick Grayson. Before Tim Drake became Robin, Dick had been the Boy Wonder. Eventually, he had decided to create his own identity, separate from Batman. He'd struck out on his own, as Nightwing.

"I'm sure Nightwing and I will cross paths someday. I did speak with Drake, however," Batman reported. "He seems clean. But I've got one more lead to check out.

Someone with a definite grudge against Bruce Wayne." He closed the private communications frequency and increased the Batmobile's speed.

Once the Batmobile had neared the harbor, Batman leapt from the flying car. His boot jets kicked on, and the Future Knight slowly descended to the waterfront. Within moments, he reached an enormous yacht with a single word painted on the side — WAYNE. The company yacht was rarely used by the man for whom it was named. However, other Wayne Enterprises executives often took advantage of the luxury it afforded.

Batman reached the ship's main cabin and secured his magnetic boots to an outside wall. Peering through a window, he spotted Jordan Pryce and several of the Jokerz gang inside — just as he'd suspected. Activating his hidden fingertip microphone, he pressed his gloved hand against the glass and listened intently to the conversation going on inside the cabin.

"We're here to talk business, Pryce," snarled Chucko, moving menacingly toward the executive.

"Our business is concluded," Pryce responded arrogantly. He was not about to be bullied. "I gave you the security codes at the Wayne Enterprises complex so you could get into the lab and take what you needed. You got the equipment you wanted." Pryce gestured at the other gang members. "While, in return, these bunglers tried — unsuccessfully, I might add — to get rid of Wayne for me."

Chucko stared at Pryce, who was casually pouring himself a glass of champagne. To secure his attention, Chucko roughly grabbed the bottle and tossed it out the cabin's window. "Word is that Wayne's not gonna make it," he announced.

"That means you get to stay top dog at Wayne Enterprises," Dee-Dee cackled.

"And everyone's happy!" the other Dee-Dee added, finishing her sister's thought.

"So why are you here?" Pryce asked, growing uneasy, forcing a smile.

"The big guy who put us in contact has decided that you're a loose end," Chucko explained.

"And loose ends should be tied up," Ghoul added, stepping in front of Pryce.

Pryce stood up to run, but Ghoul grabbed him. "Let me go!" Pryce shouted.

Ghoul slammed Pryce back into a chair and held him in place while the Dee-Dees tied him up. Then Ghoul squeezed a skull-shaped metal ring on his finger, activating a communications link. "We got him, boss," Ghoul reported.

"Better get out of there, kiddies," said a voice from the ring. "Things are about to start popping."

Leaving Pryce, the Jokerz ran for the door and yanked it open — only to find Batman blocking their way.

"No one's leaving until I get answers," the Future Knight announced.

Woof stepped toward Batman, growling.

"Not now, you idiot!" Chucko shouted at the beast. "Forget about him! We've got to get off this boat!" The Jokerz turned and bolted across the cabin, leaping through the windows. Scrambling into their flying Joker car, they sped away from the yacht.

Batman untied Pryce and pulled him out onto the yacht's deck. Suddenly, brilliant light filled the night sky and spread across the yacht.

"What's happening?" Pryce shouted, shielding his eyes.

"Hang on!" Batman yelled, grabbing Pryce around the waist. His boot jets flared, and the Future Knight sped away from the yacht, with Pryce in tow.

Just then a streak of energy stabbed down from the night sky, slamming into the yacht. The multimillion-dollar boat exploded into pieces, scattering across the harbor.

The blast sent out a shock wave that jolted Batman and Pryce, sending them tumbling. Adjusting the power on his boot jets, Batman regained control and glided softly

93

toward the dock. A police hover-cruiser pulled up beside them and two police officers leapt out. "We saw the explosion," one of them explained.

"You can ask Mr. Pryce here about that," Batman said.

"Me?" Pryce asked innocently. "I had nothing to do with it."

"Is that right?" Batman replied, activating an audio device hidden in the wrist of his suit.

Pryce's voice came from a small speaker.

"I gave you the security codes at the Wayne Enterprises complex so you could get into the lab and take what you needed. You got the equipment you wanted. While, in return, these bunglers tried — unsuccessfully, I might add — to get rid of Wayne for me."

"I want my lawyer," Pryce said as one of the officers led him to the cruiser.

A small recording chip containing the entire conversation popped into Batman's gloved hand. "I think the commissioner would like to hear this, too," he said, handing the chip to the other officer.

Then Batman blasted off the dock and disappeared back into the night.

CHAPTER ELEVEN

Deep within the Batcave, Terry scrolled through list after list on the Batcomputer's huge monitor. He had been at it all night. Finally, he dropped his head down onto his folded arms and sighed. "I'm spent," he moaned. "Every lead I try goes facedown, and the Joker's still out there."

Terry leaned over and scratched Ace behind the ears. "I don't know, pup," he muttered. "If I was the Batman I'm supposed to be, I'd have cracked this by now." He glanced around at the wreckage in the Batcave, still in shambles from the night of the Joker's attack. Then he looked back at the monitor. "I would have punched exactly the right data into the computer, or remembered that one little clue that everyone else overlooked."

"It's rarely that simple," said a deep voice from behind him.

Terry jumped to his feet and whirled around to see Bruce struggling to make his way down the stairs. Dressed in a robe and leaning heavily on his cane, the older man slowly entered the Batcave.

"How are you feeling?" Terry asked, both surprised and relieved at the sight of his mentor.

"Lousy," Bruce groaned, sitting down at the Batcomputer. Ace stood up and rested his head on his master's lap, his tail wagging happily as Bruce gently rubbed the top of his head.

Terry picked up the shredded Robin costume. "Barbara told me what the Joker did to Tim Drake," Terry revealed.

"So now you know why I didn't want you to go up against him," Bruce replied. "Impostor or not."

"But I'm a completely different Batman," Terry pleaded. "I was never a Robin." Then he paused and looked at the other costumes in the shattered glass case. "The Joker smashed all these cases, but went out of his way to destroy only the Robin suit."

Bruce smiled. "Robin *did* shoot him."

"A ghost out for revenge?" Terry shook his head. "I don't buy it. I talked to Drake. He's got no love for this costume. I can't be sure, but I think he's somehow behind this."

"That's crazy," Bruce replied, anger showing in his voice. Ace's ears perked up at the change in his master's tone.

"So was Drake," Terry reminded Bruce. "At one time, at least." Terry walked back to the computer and punched in a command. "Here's a list of everything we know the Jokerz have stolen." A list of equipment popped onto the screen. "Now let's combine these items into something that would be used by a communications expert like Tim Drake."

Terry typed in a few more commands, and 3-D images of individual pieces of equipment moved across the screen, forming a high-tech control console.

Bruce nodded grimly as he watched the console take shape. "A satellite-jamming system," he announced. "Whoever uses this can access satellite defense systems and fire them at will."

"Someone already has," Terry informed Bruce, the pieces of the puzzle starting to come together. He recounted the events that had taken place on the yacht earlier that evening, including the laser blast that destroyed the boat. "Pryce hired the Jokerz gang to get rid of you. And he paid them with the security codes to the Wayne Enterprises complex. That's how they got in to steal the equipment they needed to build this little beauty." Terry pointed at the 3-D image of the console on the monitor. "I gave the evidence to the cops to give to Barbara."

"You don't think Pryce could have been impersonating the Joker, do you?" Bruce asked skeptically.

"I used to," Terry replied. "That's why I tracked him to the yacht in the first place. But the Jokerz were there to get rid of him, tie up their boss's loose ends, they said. I got Pryce off the boat just before someone blasted it to splinters with that satellite beam."

Terry tossed the Robin costume onto the computer console. Bruce picked it up and looked at it sadly. "I hate to say it," Terry continued, "but I think your little Robin may have turned into a bitter old crow. He's got to be the brains behind this new Joker. I know it's harsh, but who else is there?"

Bruce's lips pressed tightly against each other. His whole face seemed to grow hard. For an instant, he looked every one of his seventy-seven years, and maybe a bit more. "Suit up," he ordered. "Take the car and check it out. I'll monitor you from here."

Terry smiled. He grabbed the Batsuit and headed off to change. "What happened to leaving it to the cops?" he asked, unable to resist giving Bruce just one small dig.

"Not their game," Bruce replied confidently, the old light coming back into his eyes. The hunt was on, and he was part of it once again.

"Oh," Terry stopped short, remembering something.

"There's someone I'd like to take with me." He looked right at Ace and whistled. The dog jumped to his feet, tail wagging. He glanced at his master, who nodded. Then the dog bounded to the Batmobile.

Batman silently pushed the skylight open and stared down at Tim Drake. Drake sat at a computer console in his lab, intently involved in his work. Batman gently glided to the floor. "Drake," he said calmly. "I know you're the connection to the Joker."

Batman reached out to tap Drake on the shoulder, but his hand passed right through the body. "Hologram," Batman muttered.

The image vanished. Suddenly, every door and window in the place locked automatically. Batman looked up and saw small laser blasters emerging from openings in the ceiling, all around the room. He was trapped. A wall-sized computer monitor flared to life, and a huge image of the Joker's smiling face filled the screen.

"You guessed it, Batfake!" the Joker cackled. "Mr. Drake is indeed in my employ."

The Joker's face shrank down while the image of an armored defense satellite floating through space filled the rest of the screen. "This handy little laser-armed gadget belongs to Uncle Sam," the Joker explained. "It's quite handy for shooting down enemy missiles or giving some-one a world-class hotfoot. Over the past few weeks my Jokerz have stolen the parts I needed to take control of the gizmo. Bruce's pal Timmy provided me with the final piece of the puzzle — the communications code — so now I control the satellite and its lovely little laser."

The Joker reached for a jar of Jolly Jack jelly beans, popped a piece of candy into his mouth, and continued. "Destroying the yacht was just a test shot. I can assure you, I have something special planned for dear old Gotham."

The main image on the monitor changed to a computer simulation of lasers streaking down from the sky, blowing up targets all around the city. When the destruction was complete, Batman saw that the Joker had carved a giant smiley face into Gotham. Then the Joker's face once again filled the screen. "Try and stop me if you like," he offered, "but I don't think that's going to happen anytime soon. Toodles." The screen went blank.

Batman dashed to the door. A laser blast grazed his shoulder. He ran to a window, but again the automated targeting system tracked his movements and fired a blast. He managed to duck that one. Everywhere he turned, the laser system found him. He moved to another window and was struck by a blast.

"McGinnis!" a voice shouted in his head. It was Bruce Wayne communicating with him through the Batsuit. Bruce was watching Batman's actions through the suit's eye lenses. *"You've got to take out the laser targeting system!"*

Batman flicked a Batarang into his hand, then tossed it at one of the laser blasters mounted in the ceiling. Targeting the spinning disc, the weapon shot the Batarang out of the air. Again Batman called for a Batarang, but again the laser system found its target and destroyed it.

Maybe I can use the system against itself, thought the Future Knight. He flung two Batarangs simultaneously into the air, sending each one spinning toward a side wall of the room. The laser tracked the Batarangs and blasted away, ripping a hole in one of the metal walls, exposing the system's wiring. With a soft underhand lob, Batman tossed a grenade into the tangled mass of wires and ducked out of the way.

THOOOOM!!

The grenade blasted the circuitry. The lasers shut down immediately. Firing his boot jets, Batman flew up through the window, smashing the glass and landing on the roof. Hitting a control on the Batsuit's Utility Belt, he watched the Batmobile drop from the sky. The bottom slid open and Batman leapt into the cockpit.

Ace barked happily at Batman's return. "Miss me?" the

Future Knight asked as the Batmobile streaked through the sky.

"Computer, search for the name 'Jolly Jack,'" Batman ordered, recalling the name on the Joker's jar of candy.

A holographic map of Gotham popped into the air in front of Batman, showing the location of the Jolly Jack Candy Company. The map also indicated that the company had been closed for many years. "An abandoned candy factory," Batman snickered. "Just his style."

He immediately contacted Bruce. "Wayne, I've got something. Download this map and tell Barbara to send her men to that address. I'm going to —"

Static and feedback blasted through the Batmobile's communications system. The map dissolved and the Joker's face appeared on the small screen of the Batmobile's dashboard.

"Joker!" shouted Batman, startled by the intrusion.

"Aren't you the nasty tattletale," the Joker snarled, "ratting me out to the cops before I've had my fun. Now I'm going to have to teach you a lesson!"

A brilliant light poured into the Batmobile. Batman recognized its sickening glow from the laser blast at the yacht. Accelerating the Batmobile, he just narrowly escaped the deadly beam as it tore through trees and cars.

The Batmobile was rocked by the force of the explosions. Batman, however, managed to control the speeding vehicle as Ace whined his displeasure.

"I know, boy!" he shouted. "Hang on."

Laser blasts rained down from the sky on all sides of the Batmobile. Batman flew the speeding craft through a maze of destruction as buildings shattered around him and terrified pedestrians scrambled for cover.

The Joker's grinning face glared out at Batman from the Batmobile's screen. "It's a do-it-yourself demolition derby!" the Joker roared with uncontrollable laughter. Then he broke out in a sweat and panted for breath. "I'd better sit down before I bust a gut. Catch you later, kiddo." Then the screen went dark and the laser fire stopped.

"I'm going after him!" Batman announced to Bruce as the Batmobile dove toward the street below. The Jolly Jack candy factory was just ahead. Reducing his speed, Batman glided to the factory's roof — where Chucko was waiting with a laser weapon.

THOOM! THOOM! THOOM!

Chucko fired blast after blast at the Batmobile. Batman dodged the first streaking bolt of laser fire, then the second. The third shot found its target.

The Batmobile plunged toward the rooftop, heading straight for Chucko. The terrified clown jumped out of the way as the falling vehicle smashed into a chimney. It skid-

103

ded across the roof, crashing through the factory's skylights, and finally slammed to a stop in the building's main room.

Hydraulic lifts powered open the Batmobile's canopy and the Future Knight leapt out, landing in a ready crouch beside the battered vehicle.

Woof sprang from the shadows, fangs bared and claws gleaming. Just before the crazed mutant reached him, Batman called out, "Ace!" Instantly the powerful Doberman jumped from the Batmobile, landing on top of Woof. The genetically altered gang member was no match for Bruce Wayne's muscular hound. Woof turned and ran, with Ace barking and snapping at his heels.

Batman smiled. "Good bad dog!" he said. Then, without looking, he lifted his fist to shoulder level and knocked Ghoul — who had been sneaking up behind him — to the ground.

The Dee-Dees attacked next, tumbling toward Batman. Hitting the camo-mode switch on his Utility Belt, he vanished into the shadows.

"Where did he go?" asked Dee-Dee.

Batman shoved her into her sister. "Ow! Watch it!" she shouted.

"You watch it!" cried the other Dee-Dee, as her sister shoved back.

"It's him!" whined her twin. "He's invisible or something!"

The Dee-Dees kicked and punched every flicker of light they saw, hoping to nail Batman. Instead they managed to kick over a huge container of mini-jawbreakers. The tiny round candy rolled across the floor like a wave of marbles. The sisters slipped and slid along the floor, still desperately trying to find Batman.

"Looking for someone?" Batman taunted as he faded into view. The two Dee-Dees rushed at him from opposite directions. Just as they reached the spot where he was standing, Batman fired his boot jets and flew straight up. The twins crashed into each other at full speed, knocking themselves out.

"Thanks for the dance," the airborne Batman cracked. He began his search for the Joker. Soon enough, he'd found what he was looking for.

Batman came to a large metal door bearing signs that read KEEP OUT and GENIUS AT WORK. They hung sloppily, like signs nailed to the door of a kid's room. Kicking the door open, Batman cautiously stepped inside.

The room was part high-tech control room, part playroom. Toys were strewn everywhere, but the room was dominated by the massive control console that had been stolen from the Wayne Enterprises complex on the night of Bruce Wayne's party. Above it, images on video monitors showed the aftermath of destruction that had rained down on Gotham from the satellite. Burning bridges and buildings filled the screens as firefighters struggled to get the blazes under control.

"That satellite laser packs quite a wallop," Batman muttered. "You getting this, Wayne?" he asked.

"I see it," came the reply through the Batsuit's communications hookup. *"You just keep your eyes open for the Joker. And don't let your guard down — even for a second."*

Batman spotted a figure slumped over in a heap on the floor next to the control console. He turned the unconscious body over slowly.

"Tim," Bruce gasped, seeing his former partner for the first time in over thirty years.

Batman lifted Drake's body into a chair and shook him. "Get up, Drake," he said forcefully. Drake stirred and opened his eyes. "Where's the Joker?" Batman demanded.

Drake stared up at Batman, confusion in his eyes. "Joker?" he asked.

"Drop the act!" Batman shouted angrily. "I know you're working with him."

Drake stood up and walked stiffly around the room, like a man trying to shake off the effects of a bad dream. "The Joker's gone. I don't know where he is. Really."

Bruce's voice came through the Batsuit. *"The suit's sen-*

sors aren't picking up any pulse fluctuations," he reported. "He's telling the truth, Terry."

Drake shook his head. "I don't do this anymore. Boy Wonder playing the hero. Fighting the bad guys, and no one ever gets hurt." Drake suddenly dropped to one knee, overwhelmed by a horrible memory that seemed to flood his whole body. "I killed him. I didn't mean to. I tried so hard to forget, but I can still hear the shot, still see his dead smile. Every night the dreams get stronger. He's there, laughing at me, telling me that I'm just as bad as he is, that we're the same."

"I'm calling an ambulance," Batman stated flatly.

Just then Drake straightened up and smiled. An eerie calmness came over him in sharp contrast to his devastated mood of a moment ago. "No, I'm all right," he said confidently. "Forgive me, Terry. Just old, nasty memories. Nothing, really. I'm fine now."

"How do you know my name?" Batman demanded.

Drake smiled coldly, tossing a brightly colored ball from hand to hand. As he pitched it into the air, a claw popped out, attaching itself to Batman's costume. A sharp electrical charge surged through the Batsuit, and Batman collapsed to the floor, unable to move. "There's nothing about you I *don't* know, Batfake!"

"McGinnis!" Bruce cried through the Batsuit, watching helplessly.

"Hello, Bruce," Drake called out. "I know you can hear me. I'm sure you've got monkey-boy here wired for sound somehow. That's peachy. I don't want you to miss a minute of this!"

Drake's body twisted and contorted, then began to transform. His skin turned pale, then chalk white. His hair became green and oily. His limbs struck out, slamming into anything in their way. With a final shudder, the transformation was complete.

Tim Drake was gone.

And in his place stood the Joker!

CHAPTER TWELVE

"**O**h, I never get tired of that!" the Joker smirked.

Batman, still unable to move, stared up at the Joker in horror. "Drake — you're the Joker?" he asked, barely able to comprehend what he had just seen.

"Brilliant, isn't it?" the Clown Prince of Crime chirped. "And the beautiful part is that Drake, the flabby oaf, doesn't even know I'm using his body as a time-share!"

"That's not possible," Batman groaned.

"Anything is possible for a genius like me," the Joker boasted. "Old man Wayne should have told you that."

"B-but how?" Batman stammered.

"During the weeks in which I kidnapped young Drake, I encoded my magnificent DNA onto a microchip," the Joker began, clearly enjoying his moment of triumph. "I then placed the chip into bird-boy's head. Right here." The Joker turned around and parted his hair, pointing to a tiny mole. "Everything that was me was planted, like a seed, in Tim Drake's subconscious. It took a few decades to rewrite his cellular makeup, but in time I popped up again. At first I could only spend short periods of time using Drake's body. But now I can control the changes at will. Very soon I'll be strong enough to live in this body permanently. Then it's bye-bye, Timmy, and hello, Joker!"

Batman struggled to make sense of it all as he fought to free his arms from the pulsating claw that kept him immobile.

"Thanks to this little satellite hookup, my comeback party is going to set the town on fire," the Joker announced. "Now, where shall I strike? Gotham General Hospital, where your dear little girlfriend Dana is recuperating? Or maybe the happy garden of Mrs. Mary McGinnis?"

The Joker pressed two buttons on his control panel, and the images on the monitors changed. One showed the hospital, another pictured Terry's mom and little brother working in a garden outside their apartment building. "Ah, but the answer is obvious," the Joker cooed, pressing another button. A third monitor switched to an image of Wayne Manor. "The one and only kickoff point must be stately Wayne Manor. But don't worry, we'll be hitting those other spots soon enough."

The Joker squatted down and grinned right at Batman, sensing that Bruce Wayne was watching his every move. "Bye-bye, Brucie," the Joker said. "I guess I should salute you as a worthy adversary for all those years, but the truth is . . . I really hate your guts! What about it, kid?" he snarled, directing his question to Batman. "Any last words for the old Batfart?"

Batman's eyes narrowed and he nodded. "Yeah," he grunted. "Sic 'im, doggie!"

Ace bolted from the darkness, leaping right at the Joker. As the demented clown reached for the FIRE button, Ace slammed into him and knocked him to the floor.

"Ace! Here!" Batman called. Ace ran over to Batman and chomped down on the electrical restraining clamp attached to the Batsuit. The device cracked under the pressure of the Doberman's powerful jaws, then sparked and fell off.

Batman scrambled to his feet as Ace leapt at the Joker again. This time the clown was ready. He slapped the dog with an electric joy buzzer. Ace whimpered, then fell into a deep sleep.

Batman sprang at the Joker, who still held the buzzer. He slammed the Joker's hand into the keyboard on the control console. Power from the joy buzzer sent a huge surge of electric energy coursing through the system.

"No!" shouted the Joker, pulling his hand from the keyboard and tossing the buzzer aside.

Sparks flew from the console, its programming scrambled, causing the satellite to shift position and begin firing at random. The laser beam instantly struck a warehouse near the candy factory, then moved slowly toward the Joker's lair, seeking the source of its signal.

The Joker saw this on his computer monitor. "Oh, good," he snarled at Batman. "The beam's headed this way. Now I'll have to start all over again somewhere else." Then he shrugged and walked away from Batman. "Thanks for wrecking everything, kid. See ya around."

Batman reached out and grabbed the Joker. "Hold it," he ordered. "I'm taking you in."

"Right," the Joker replied, slamming an elbow into Batman with speed that shocked the Future Knight. Batman crumpled to the ground, clutching his stomach. "You're out of your league, McGinnis," the Joker declared, circling Batman. "I know every trick the original Batman and Robin knew at their peak."

Batman rolled over and sprang to his feet. "Maybe," he replied fiercely, ignoring the pain. "But you don't know a thing about me."

"What's to know?" the Joker asked mockingly. "You're a punk. An amateur. A costumed errand boy taking orders from a senile old man."

Batman turned and ran toward the door.

The Joker laughed. "That's it. Run, save yourself rather than fight. That's about your speed."

Batman slammed the door shut and broke off the knob. "Just you and me now," he announced, smiling at the Joker. "Let's dance, Bozo!" Batman dove at the Joker, knocking him to the ground. But the Joker was fast and strong. He tossed Batman away, then pounced on top of him. It seemed that for every blow Batman landed, the Joker landed two.

Batman finally broke away. Diving behind a table, he whispered into his costume's headset, "He's tough. Any suggestions, boss?"

"The Joker's vain and he likes to talk," Bruce's voice came back. *"He'll try to distract you, but don't listen. Block it out and power on through."*

"That gives me an idea," Batman said. "I like to talk, too."

While Batman and the Joker battled, the Jokerz gathered in the factory's main room.

"Look!" shouted Dee-Dee, pointing to a window. A brilliant glow from outside poured into the factory.

"The laser!" shrieked Ghoul. "It's coming this way!"

"Run for it!" yelled the other Dee-Dee.

As the Jokerz dashed outside, they saw the laser beam moving closer and closer to the factory. They also saw Commissioner Gordon and a squad of her police officers.

"Hands up!" shouted Gordon. "You're all under arrest."

"This is all *your* fault!" Dee-Dee shouted at her sister.

"*My* fault!" screamed her twin. "I'm the smart one."

"I'm sick and tired of listening to you two bicker!" Ghoul chimed in.

"Well, you'll have a long, long time in your own private jail cell, where you won't have to listen to these two," the commissioner said to Ghoul as the Jokerz were slapped into handcuffs.

"I want my own cell, too!" whined Dee-Dee, trying to kick her sister as two police officers pulled the twins away from each other, then led them into a waiting hover-cruiser.

Back in the Joker's playroom, Batman changed his strategy. The Future Knight ducked a karate blow, then kneed the Joker in the stomach.

"What are you doing?" the Joker gasped in shock.

"It's called fighting dirty," Batman replied.

"The old Batman would never —"

Batman slammed the Joker in the stomach again. "I'm not the old Batman. I told you: You don't know me."

The glow outside grew brighter, the laser inching ever closer, as the Joker swung at Batman. "Funny guy, huh?" the Joker hissed.

"Can't say the same for you," Batman taunted, ducking away from the Joker's blows.

"I've never had any complaints before," the Joker boasted, grinning.

"Or laughs, either," Batman replied.

The Joker's smile disappeared, replaced by a scowl. "Impudent brat!" he shouted, clearly shaken. "Who do you think you're talking to?"

"Not a comedian," Batman shot back. "I'll tell you that much."

"Shut up!" the Joker screamed, pulling a weapon from his jacket and aiming it at Batman.

The Future Knight activated his boot jets and zoomed up to the rafters. Tossing a Batarang down, he knocked the weapon from the Joker's hand. "The old Batman never talked to you much, did he?" Batman shouted down. "Didn't laugh at your jokes, either. That's why you kept coming back, kept coming after him. You never got a laugh out of him, and it drove you nuts."

"I don't need you to analyze me!" The Joker covered his ears and grinned nervously. "I'm not listening."

"Get a clue, Clownie!" Batman called down from the darkness above. "Wayne's got no sense of humor. He wouldn't know a good joke if it bit him on the cape. Not that *you* ever had a good joke."

"Shut up!" the Joker shrieked again. He ran to the door and tried to pull it open, but it was stuck shut.

Batman's mocking voice filled the room. "I mean, joy buzzers and squirting flowers? How lame can you get? Where's the *good* material?"

The Joker spun around, hatred glowing in his eyes. He looked up, trying to spot the shadowy figure taunting him. "Show yourself!" he demanded, his voice crazed.

Batman's laughter drifted down from the darkness. "But me — you make me laugh because you're so pathetic."

"Stop that!" the Joker cried.

Batman leapt from one section of the rafters to another, flitting across the room like a shadow. Again he laughed, this time even harder and louder. "So you fell into a tank of acid, got your skin bleached, and decided to become a super villain. Talk about lame! What's the problem? You couldn't get work as a rodeo clown?"

The Joker raced to his worktable and grabbed a handful of grenades. "Don't you dare laugh at me!" he threatened.

116

Batman's hearty laugh echoed around the cavernous room. "Why not?" he asked in a mock innocent tone. "I thought the Joker always wanted to make Batman laugh!"

"YOU'RE NOT BATMAN!" the Joker raged, tossing grenades wildly into the darkness.

THOOOM! THOOOM! FOOOM!

The grenades exploded around the room. Huge chunks of wall, ceiling, and glass shattered and crashed to the floor. The impact of the explosions knocked Batman from his hiding place among the rafters, and he hit the ground with a thud. Before Batman could get to his feet, the Joker spotted him and tossed a grenade in his direction. Batman tried to roll out of the way, but the grenade went off.

THOOOM!

The force of the explosion slammed Batman into a wall. He crumpled in a heap, groaning and struggling for breath. The Joker grabbed a worktable and flipped it over onto Batman's sprawling body. Then he pulled the mask off Terry's face.

"Come on, McGinnis!" the Joker roared. "Laugh it up now, you miserable little punk! Laugh!"

Terry's mouth opened, as if he was trying to speak.

The Joker leaned closer. "I can't hear you, Batfake!"

Terry opened his clenched fist to reveal the Joker's electric hand buzzer, which the demented clown had tossed away earlier. Terry smiled. "Ha, ha!" He slapped the buzzer onto the back of the Joker's head, right on the mole. A massive burst of electric power crackled through the buzzer and into the Joker's skull — destroying the DNA microchip.

The Joker screamed, his body twisting and shuddering. His face softened. The madness left his eyes. With a final choking gasp, he fell silent, slumping to the floor.

Batman slipped his mask back on, then pushed the table off. He leaned over the Joker's limp body and looked into the gentle eyes and exhausted face of Tim Drake.

"Where am I?" Drake asked in a tired, strained voice.

Batman smiled. "With a friend," he said softly.

Ace, fully recovered from his electric shock, barked loudly and scratched at the door. Batman helped Drake to his feet, then wrenched the door open. Glancing out a window, Batman saw the yellow streak of destruction, now only inches from the factory.

"Come on, Drake," Batman urged the ragged, limping figure beside him. "I know you've just been through a lot, but this whole building's going to go up any second, and I don't think either of us wants to be around to see it from the inside!"

Summoning whatever strength he had left, Drake threw an arm over Batman's shoulder. Then the Future Knight helped him toward the exit, with Ace close at his heels.

FOOOM!

The laser struck the candy factory, tearing a gaping hole in the roof. Debris rained down on the escaping duo.

"Look out!" Batman shouted, shielding Drake as best he could as pieces of the ceiling tumbled onto them. The Batsuit protected them from the chunks of plaster as they hurried toward the factory's exit.

Still supporting Drake's weight, Batman kicked open the front door. The flashing red lights of police vehicles cast an eerie glow in the run-down hallway, just as the laser struck the Joker's control panel.

FZZZ-THOOM!

The panel exploded, sending flames, smoke, and chunks of metal tearing through the hallway. Batman leapt through the open front door, carrying Drake, just as searing shards of metal passed only inches above his head. He hit the pavement hard, somersaulting. Ace was right behind him. Batman scrambled to his feet, protecting Drake throughout the entire acrobatic maneuver.

Commissioner Gordon raced to his side. "Are you okay?"

Batman nodded.

"How about you, Tim?" the commissioner asked, concern showing in her voice.

Tim Drake looked at her, then collapsed into Batman's arms.

"Let's get this man into an ambulance!" the commissioner shouted. "Now!"

As the emergency crew helped Drake onto a stretcher, Batman looked back at the candy factory. With the control panel destroyed, the laser weapon had shut off, effectively taking itself out of commission.

Seconds later, Commissioner Gordon turned to ask Batman a question. But the Future Knight was already gone, slipping back into the night's comforting cloak of darkness.

High above the earth, the defense satellite that had been bombarding Gotham City drifted harmlessly through the black void of space.

EPILOGUE

Gotham General was the city's biggest and finest hospital — and its busiest. Doctors moved deliberately from room to room, making their rounds. Nurses hooked up IVs and checked monitoring equipment, keeping track of their patients. Concerned friends and relatives gathered in waiting rooms, comforting and supporting one another.

In a private room on the fourth floor, Tim Drake rested comfortably. The back and sides of his head were covered in bandages. His face looked tired, but it was also serene for the first time in many years. An attractive gray-haired visitor sat near the edge of the bed and gently held his hand.

"You didn't have to cover up for me, Barbara," Drake said.

"None of this was your fault, Tim," Barbara Gordon replied affectionately. "The guy who hijacked your body is gone. You were just along for the ride."

A knock came at the door, then a handsome teenager appeared. "How are you doing, Mr. Drake?" he asked.

Barbara stood up. "Tim, this is Terry McGinnis," she said, gesturing to the young man.

Drake stared curiously at Terry.

"We met the other night," Terry explained, raising his eyebrows in a knowing way.

"We did?" Tim asked, puzzled, looking Terry up and down.

"I looked a little different, though," Terry admitted, smiling.

"Oh," Drake said, understanding. "I owe you, big-time."

"Forget it," Terry replied with a shrug.

"For what it's worth," Drake began, sitting up in bed, "Bruce couldn't have chosen anyone better to wear the costume."

Terry smiled and shook Drake's hand. "Coming from you, that means everything."

Drake nodded and settled back into his bed. "Sometimes the important things go unsaid," he stated, exhaustion and a bit of regret coloring his voice. "If there's one thing I've learned, it's that you've got to appreciate the people in your life while you have the chance."

Barbara leaned over and took Drake's hand again. She smiled sadly, knowing exactly what he meant. "Not everyone is capable of expressing that, Tim," she explained softly. "No matter how much they might feel it in their heart."

"I know," Drake replied.

A sound at the door caused everyone to turn their heads in that direction. Terry stepped over and pulled the door open. "Bruce!" he exclaimed. "What are you doing here?"

Bruce Wayne, his cane grasped firmly in his right hand, entered the room. "It's where I should be," he said to Terry. He started toward Tim, then stopped and looked back at Terry. "I've been thinking about something you told me," he said. "And you were wrong. It's not Batman that makes *you* worthwhile, it's the other way around. Never tell yourself anything different."

Terry smiled at his mentor. "Thanks, Bruce," was all he said. It was all he needed to say.

Bruce slowly crossed the room to Tim's bedside. "Hello, Tim," he said warmly.

Tim Drake looked up at the man who had meant so much to him so long ago, and the gulf between them, widened by a thirty-five-year separation, vanished. "Hi, old man," he replied, extending his hand. Bruce took it, then grasped his shoulder.

Terry knew it was time to leave. He quietly backed out

of the room, leaving Bruce, Tim, and Barbara Gordon alone. There was a lot of history between them, and lots to catch up on. Moving quickly down the hospital hallway, he made his way to another patient's room. His heart beat a bit more quickly, as it always did when he thought about seeing Dana.

At this point in his life Terry knew that he had a handle on being Batman. But he also knew that he still needed to work on being Terry McGinnis — boyfriend, son, and brother. *"Everything in good time,"* he could still hear his father say. The true meaning of those words had never been clearer.

Terry McGinnis may never have had it easy, but he wouldn't want it any other way.

ABOUT THE AUTHOR

MICHAEL TEITELBAUM has been a writer, editor, and packager of children's books, comic books, and magazines for more than twenty years. He has worked on staff as an editor at Gold Key Comics, Golden Books, Putnam/ Grosset, and Macmillan.

Michael's packaging company, Town Brook Press, created and packaged *Spider-Man Magazine*, a monthly publication, for Marvel Entertainment. Recently, Town Brook Press has been creating sports and entertainment sticker collections for Panini S.p.A. of Italy.

Some of Michael's more recent writing includes *Garfield: Pet Force* books (a series of five titles); *Breaking Barriers: In Sports, In Life* (based on the life of Jackie Robinson); and *Extreme Pokémon*, all published by Scholastic; *Wimzie's House* storybooks, published by Carson-Dellosa; and *NASCAR Super Racers*, published by HarperCollins.

THE FIRST FEATURE-LENGTH
BATMAN BEYOND MOVIE

COMING ONLY TO VIDEO AND DVD
OCTOBER 31, 2000